Charles Gavan Duffy

Short Life of Thomas Davis

Charles Gavan Duffy

Short Life of Thomas Davis

ISBN/EAN: 9783337057800

Printed in Europe, USA, Canada, Australia, Japan

Cover: Foto ©Raphael Reischuk / pixelio.de

More available books at **www.hansebooks.com**

SHORT LIFE

OF

THOMAS DAVIS

1840—1846

BY

SIR CHARLES GAVAN DUFFY

" Those who live as models for the mass
Are singly of more value than they all.
Keep but the model safe, new men will rise
To take its mould, and other days to prove
How great a good was Luria's having lived."

BROWNING

London
T. FISHER UNWIN
PATERNOSTER SQUARE

Dublin
SEALY, BRYERS & WALKER
MIDDLE ABBBY STREET
MDCCCXCV

CONTENTS.

SHORT LIFE OF THOMAS DAVIS.

CHAPTER I.

THE STUDENT. 1831-1838.

HOMAS DAVIS, the most notable Irishman of the generation to which he belonged, was born in Mallow, County Cork, on the 14th of October, 1814, When he came into the world Ireland was a garrison, in the same sense that Calcutta or Gibraltar is a garrison to-day. The native population, who were universally Catholics, amounted to between six and seven millions, but none of them under the existing

B

law could occupy any office of authority in their native country. In the town where he was born there was some form of municipal government, but the administrators were exclusively Protestants. There was an Established Church, maintained at the common cost of the whole population, for a minority of less than one in a dozen, and more profusely endowed than any establishment in Christendom. The only schools supported or recognized by the State were under exclusively Protestant management. Justice was administered in courts in which the entire official staff were of the favoured creed. And the recognized test of what was called "loyalty" was the determination to perpetuate Protestant ascendancy in the Church, the executive government, the magistracy and the municipalities. Ireland was represented by a hundred members in the parliament of London, but only Protestants could be elected. The peerage, with half a dozen exceptions, lived in England, and the resident gentry and professional classes led gay convivial lives, with little thought of politics beyond the necessary precautions to keep the populace quiet. A few prosperous Catholics, in the mercantile or professional classes in Dublin, demanded civil and religious liberty from time to time; but the Protestants who sympathized with them were scarcely more numerous than the

Indian officials to-day who would manumit the
Hindoo.

Davis belonged by birth to the minority who
enjoyed the monopoly of property and power. His
father, James Thomas Davis, was a surgeon in the
Royal Artillery ; his mother, Mary Atkins, was the
descendent of a good Anglo-Irish family, which traced
back its line to the great Norman House of Howard,
and—what Davis loved better, to remember—to the
great Celtic House of O'Sullivan Beare. I found
among his papers this fragment of a letter, in his own
handwriting, which probably tells all the reader will
care to know on the subject :—

"My father was a gentleman of Welsh blood, but his
family had been so long settled in England that they
were, and considered themselves, English. He held
a commission in the English army. I am descended
on my mother's side from a Cromwellian settler whose
descendants, though they occasionally intermarried with
Irish families, continued Protestants, and in the English interest, and suffered for it in 1688. I myself was
brought up High Tory and an Episcopalian Protestant,
and if I am no longer a Tory it is from conviction, for
all those nearest and dearest to me are so still."

This mixture of Celtic and Norman blood is an
amalgam which has nourished noble fruit. Nearly
a hundred years earlier, a father of Anglo-Norman
descent and a mother of pure Celtic strain reared a
son who ranks with Bacon and Milton in the in-

tellectual hierarchy of these Islands, and many noted
Irishmen are of the same mixed race as Edmund
Burke.

Davis was born after his father's death, the youngest
of four children. When he was four years of age the
family removed to Dublin, living at Warrington Place
till 1830, and afterwards at 61 (now 67) Lower
Baggot Street. His birthplace was a garden of traditional and historical romance but he left Mallow so
early that it would be fanciful to speak of boyish
impressions at an age when he was scarcely breeched.
He was educated at the noted school of Mr. Mongan,
Lower Mount Street, and in 1831 entered Trinity
College. As a child he was feeble and delicate;
and in youth he was subject to frequent fits of despondency—less an individual trait, I fancy, than an
not uncommon result of the poetic temperament.
But when he became a student of Trinity all symptoms
of debility had disappeared; he was fond of long
walking excursions, and entered almost immediately
on the systematic study which needs a solid reserve of
vigour to sustain. His boyhood passed as the boyhood of poets and thinkers is apt to pass; he was
silent, thoughtful, and self-absorbed. We hear, without surprise, that the boisterous spirits of schoolboys
oppressed him, and that he took slight pleasure in
their sports; for this is the common lot of his class.

So little is known with certainty of that period, that I must borrow from a former book the few particulars I was able to gather from his contemporaries :—

"One of his kinswomen, resident in Melbourne, who judged him as the good people judged who mistook the young swan for an ugly duck, assured me that he was a dull child. He could scarcely be taught his letters, and she often heard the school-boy stuttering through 'My Name is Norval' in a way that was pitiable to see. When he had grown up, if you asked him the day of the month, the odds were he could not tell you. He never was any good at handball or hurling, and knew no more than a fool how to take care of the little money his father left him. She saw him more than once in tears listening to a common country fellow playing old airs on a fiddle, or sitting in a drawing-room as if he were dazed when other young people were enjoying themselves ; which facts, I doubt not, are authentic, though the narrator somewhat mistook their significance. Milton, in painting his own inspired youth, has left a picture which will be true for ever of the class of which he was a chief :—

"'When I was yet a child, no childish play
  To me was pleasing; all my mind was set
  Serious to learn and know; and thence to do
  What might be public good : myself I thought
  Born to that end—born to promote all truth,
  All righteous things.' "*

He lived a life of day-dreams for the most part— the first and most subtle discipline of a boy of genius. He has told us the subject of his reveries.

---

* *Young Ireland*, chap. iii.

"What thoughts were mine in early youth! like some
    old Irish song,
Brimful of love and life and truth, my spirit gushed
    along.
I hope to right my native isle, to win a soldier's fame,
I hoped to rest in woman's smile, and win a minstrel's
    name."

When he entered college, in his seventeenth year,
we do not pass at once from obscurity to light; his
fellow-students or teachers had nothing to tell of that
era, except that he was habitually self-absorbed and
a prodigious reader. For four or five years he hiber-
nated among his books, slowly gathering knowledge
and silently framing opinions. From his casual talk
he was regarded as a Benthamite, a dumb questioner
of authority, discontented with many things established, but not likely to prove a formidable opponent.
In 1836, when he was keeping his last term as a law
student in London, one of his early friends saw with
amazement silent tears fall down his cheeks at some
generous allusion to the Irish character on the stage
—a sensibility he was far from expecting in the supposed Utilitarian.

Though Trinity College was the amphitheatre where
young athletes were trained to defend Protestant
ascendancy, it has always reared passionate Nationalists. There is scarcely a man distinguished as an
opponent of British supremacy, from Jonathan Swift

to Isaac Butt, who was not educated in that institution. In 1793 two of its graduates, Thomas Emmet
and Wolfe Tone, first taught nakedly the doctrine,
that the essential basis of Irish liberty was peace and
brotherhood among Protestants and Catholics. And
when Davis matriculated, there was a little knot of
generous Protestants in college who talked to each
other the old doctrine of Tone and Emmet—Ireland,
not for a sect or a caste, but for the whole Irish
people. Thomas Wallis, a college tutor, Torrens
McCullagh,* a young barrister of great colloquial
powers, and Francis Kearney, a student, who died
before he was called to the Bar, were the leading
spirits in this connection. For a time these young
men barely knew Davis, and, as I learned from the
survivor, they misunderstood him so completely that
one of the set fixed upon him a nickname implying
contented mediocrity. They always insisted that his
nature had not then awakened, and that there was no
hint in his conversation of the fountain of thought
and passion soon to overflow, or of the indomitable
will masked under habitual silence.

That his fellow-students misjudged Davis's natural
endowments became plain enough to themselves in
the end ; but I think they misjudged as completely

---

* Known in latter times as McCullagh Torrens, M.P.

his opinions when they knew him first. His writings, when he came to write, furnish evidence difficult to resist that his voluminous studies were guided by a purpose from an early period. While the young men about him were dreaming, as the goal of life, to win the great seal or episcopal lawn, this silent student had a rarer and more daring ambition. He resolved to be the servant of his country, as the great men of old who touched his heart had been. If he devoured history, and the historical romance and drama which light up the past, and pondered on codes and annals, it was that he might not be an unprofitable servant. The foundations of character are laid in youth; and in his verses, where we may most confidently seek the secrets of a poet's heart, he tells us how early the hope of serving Ireland began: "when boyhood's fire was in his blood" he read of Leonidas and Thermopylæ, and how Horatius and his comrades held the Sublician Bridge, and prayed that he too might be worthy to do some gallant deed for his country.

"And from that time, through wildest woe,
   THAT HOPE has shone, a far light;
Nor could love's brightest summer glow
   Outshine that solemn starlight:

It seemed to watch above my head
   In forum, field, and fane;
Its angel voice sang round my bed,
   'A NATION ONCE AGAIN.'"

He sat down before the chaos of Irish annals confused by honest ignorance and distorted by industrious malice, determined to understand the story of his native country. So far as we know there was no friendly hand to lead him through this pathless thicket. Fortunate is the youth who has a guide fit to make plain the difficult, and to light the obscure, tracts of his study. But is he not stronger and more sure-footed in the end who has made his way across impediments and through the gloom by his native force? This silent labour was a discipline for life, and laid the foundations of a consummate man. In his little den in college, apart from the babble of local politics, he studied the Irish problem in the abstract. He saw in the island all the natural capacity and resources for self-government. Nature had furnished the first conditions and essential equipments for a great emporium of commercial enterprise to this land of multitudinous rivers and harbours, lying between two rich continents. The native race had proved their capacity in early civilization and early commerce, and by workmanship of marvellous beauty, before the base jealousy of a stronger neighbour had brought them to ruin. Their exiles in later times had won distinction in war, diplomacy, and the art of government, and there was no reason to fear that the native sap had dried up. The people were generous, pious, and romantic, vigilant husbandmen and skilled artisans, and would be fortified by the mettle of harder races; for the Ireland he dreamed of restoring was one in which native-born men, of whatever origin, should unite as Irishmen, as the Briton, the Angle, the Dane, the Norman, and the Netherlander had united in England. It was in this spirit he approached the Irish Tories :—

> "What matter that at different shrines
>   We pray unto one God—
> What matter that at different times
>   Your fathers won this sod—
> In fortune and in name we're bound
>   By stronger links than steel;
> And neither can be safe nor sound
>   But in the other's weal."

A man of genius commonly attributes an inordinate importance to the mind which gave his own an impulse at a critical period of development. Very often it is a mind inferior to his own, but he is slow to perceive and loth to acknowledge this fact. Coleridge had such a feeling towards Bowles and Landor towards Southey, and Davis had certainly such a feeling towards Wallis. Wallis's position among his associates bore a not remote resemblance to that of Coleridge among the Lake Poets. He projected on a prodigious scale, but he made no attempt to perform what he projected. A thinker who does not work is not necessarily a wasted force. His talk was full of new, startling, and often audacious truths ; he had the gift of inspiring thought and awakening feeling, and, like his great exemplar, he considered his function exhausted when he had exhorted a man to do some good work, without any intention of setting him the example. One of his half-scoffing admirers used to say that if you could work miracles or were willing to try, and ready to be bullied for having failed, Wallis had a fascinating series of prodigies at your service. But to the serious mind of Davis these wild coruscations were like the electric current smiting the dusky coil of wire. They kindled his faculties for action, and inflamed his slumbering imagination. Wallis frankly accepted the hypothesis that he was the fire-bearer. Not long after Davis's death, he wrote to me—

"You must consider all the experience I have had for the ten years or so that I was 'Professor of Things in general and Patriotism in particular,' in a garret in T.C.D. If I, and surely it was I that did it (his exorbitantly extravagant praise of me showed it), if I loosed the tenacious phlegm that clogged Davis's nature and hid his powers from himself and the world—if I kept Torrens McCullagh for several years from deflecting into a Whig parabola, which was his natural tendency—and if I changed John Dillon from a Whig and Utilitarian to a Nationalist and a popular leader—I must have expended rather a serious amount of magnetic force in the task, to say nothing of the scores of others that I mesmerized with less success, or less remarkable results."

In the society of these young men and their friends
the knowledge Davis had gathered got classified by
friendly discussion, and opinions which were in solution became crystallized.

A debating society is the natural training school of
ambitious students, but at this time there was no such
society in the University, and an extern Historical
Society, composed chiefly of college students, which
had trained a generation in logic and rhetoric, had
recently ceased to meet. In the beginning of 1839 a
new College Historical Society was founded. The
original members consisted of ten Conservatives and
ten Liberals ; there was as yet no talk of Nationalists.
The third name in the list was that of Thomas Davis,
the preceding ones being John Thomas Ball, since
Lord Chancellor of Ireland, and Joseph LeFanu, afterwards distinguished as a popular novelist.

Addresses were delivered at the opening of the
Society's session in November, and at the close in
June. And Davis who became auditor, equivalent to
president, delivered the closing address in June, 1840.

It was in the Society he made the acquaintance of
a man to whom, in later years, he was accustomed to
open his whole mind and heart—Daniel Owen
Maddyn. Forty years ago, when I first meditated
writing a memoir of Davis, Maddyn sent me as a
contribution to it his recollections of his friend at this

period, and his impression of the young men among whom he lived.*

"I first knew Thomas Davis in the early part of the year 1838. He had, a short time previously, published a pamphlet on 'The Reform of the House of Lords '—a subject which, in those palmy days of Whig-Radicalism, attracted much attention. One evening, seated by the side of Thomas MacNevin, I saw a short thickset young man, wrapped in a fear-nought coat, shamble into the room, and speak in a tone between jest and earnest to several of the members. 'That,' said MacNevin, ' is Davis.'† 'What! was it he wrote the pamphlet on Peerage Reform ?' 'Ay, yonder you behold the cataract that is to sweep away the House of Lords.' There was something about Davis which I liked at first sight. There was a frank honesty about his face, and I liked his large well-opened eyes.

"The Historical Society used to assemble at Radley's Hotel, in a large room upstairs. A temporary bar was placed across the room, inside of which were the members, who used to muster to the number of thirty or thereabouts, and have an audience of visitors double

---

* Since his death, his kinsman, Denny Lane, has given me the correspondence which, during the entire period of his public career, Davis maintained with Maddyn. Maddyn became author of the *Age of Pitt and Fox*, *Leaders of Opinion*, and some other notable books. He spelt his name originally Madden, but in later years adopted the other form in his books and correspondence.

† "Poor MacNevin! He was far the wittiest man in the Society, he was a favourite of all parties, and he was an admirable elocutionist. He was a pupil of Vandendoff; he had great power of artistic assumption of a *rôle* in speaking. He was then in the tide of spirits, buoyant with hope. His sarcasm was poignant, and clean cutting."

that number. The style of speaking was vicious in the
extreme, showy, declamatory, and vehement. The arts
of elocution were little studied. Fluency and vehemence were the objects aimed at. To astound, not to
persuade, was the aim of nine-tenths of the speakers.
It was necessarily, therefore, a bad school of eloquence,
and was suited to produce only platform speakers.

"But there was much about the society which was
attractive. Cloistered students rubbed off against its
walls their rust and pedantry. College rivals became
friends in its social circle; men of opposite sentiments
became acquainted; and friendly intercourse was promoted amongst those who were afterwards to meet in
scenes of real competition. After the violent speeches
there were excellent suppers, and members forgot over
broiled bones the belabouring they had inflicted upon
each other.

"Davis made no figure in this society. His solid
massive talents were not adapted for the light clever
fencing of the wordy disputants. But he liked the
society on the principle that anything amongst young
men was better than intellectual stagnation. He was
elected Auditor, whose office was to manage its affairs
and keep the members together.

"He had no 'name' as a speaker, but he was respected as a man of talents. His moral qualities, however, were not appreciated, chiefly because, up to that
time (his twenty-fourth year), he had not openly de-
veloped all his character. It certainly did not redound
much to the discrimination of his associates that his
merits were not earlier recognized. The general opinion
of him was that he was 'a book in breeches.'

"In college he read for honours, solely for the sake
of exercising his mind and training it to intellectual
discipline. The Rev. Samuel Butcher, F.T.C.D., was

the examiner, and he said that he never heard better answering. The candidates were men of great talents, and were laboriously prepared by 'grinders.' Davis, however, read by himself, and he had no recourse to professional assistants in preparing himself for the examination. Few things were more effective in forming his high-toned character than his ethical studies. They made him a strong thinker, and gave him large and noble views of mankind. Of all the moral philosophers Bishop Butler was his favourite. He placed him above all the others for originality and grandeur of views. If my memory does not deceive me he once called Butler 'the Newton of Ethics.'

"He was a Church of England man of the older and more liberal school. He was a frequent reader of the divines of the seventeenth century; the writings of Jeremy Taylor were heartily appreciated by him. He had at times a bold manner of putting his thoughts, which might mislead an ignorant person; but no man was more averse than he from licentious philosophy, or from profane discourse. I never recollect him speaking with levity on serious subjects. His frame of mind was naturally reverent, and the authors whom he habitually read were not of the mocking school. But when little men of little minds sought to strengthen their weak powers by allying themselves with fanaticism he would expose their follies in a trenchant style, against which the refuted fanatic or convicted TARTUFFE would defend himself by crying out with dissembled fright, 'Irreligious!

"He was at that time as delightful a young man as it was possible to meet with in any country. He was much more joyous than at the time he became immersed in practical politics. His cheerfulness was not so much the result of temperament as of his sanguine philosophy,

and of his wholesome, happy views of life. The sources
of enjoyment were abundant to a man of his large
faculties, highly cultured possessing withal a body which
supplied him with vigour and energy.

"In his politics he was what would be called a hearty
Liberal. There was a close juncture between the Irish
and English politicians, and like most of his contemporaries, Davis for the time chimed in indifferently well
with the Liberal party.

"On comparing him with his associates in the College
Historical Society, and with the other collegians of his
own standing whom I remember, two things especially
distinguished him. First the plainness of his character,
and the perfect simplicity of his manners. I speak the
plain truth when I declare that, from what I could see
of Davis at the time, he was altogether free from affec-
tation of every kind, and from all petty personal vanity.
He had nothing of the showy air and varnished pretensions of others. No man could be less of a coxcomb.
Vanities of appearance he utterly despised. He really
was what he seemed to be.

"The second point in which he differed from his contemporaries was in the vastly extended course of his
reading. He was a constant reader of history—of
modern travels—of the biography of authors—and of the
text writers in politics, such as Bolingbroke and Burke.
Add to this that he had not, like others, neglected his
college business. He had, besides, read some of the
chief works in legal science.

"He read from pure thirst for knowledge, with a spirit
of moral enthusiasm akin to the ardour of a brave
mariner, like Cook, voyaging to seek new countries.
He plunged into an ocean of reading, trusting to his
mental elasticity and thought for floating buoyantly
under a deeply laden memory."

With these reminiscences of his college career the life of the student may close; that of the man of profound thought and decisive action was about to begin.

We can see through Maddyn's eyes the young auditor of the Historical Society among his associates, but he has not lifted the curtain from a more touching and impressive figure, the young student in his college cell. Secluded, unrecognized, and knowing himself only by casual flashes of insight, he was probably supremely happy because he was possessed by the passion which is more engrossing to the boy of genius than love of power or the love of women to manhood—the love of knowledge. He had access to a boundless library, the noble gateway to all the treasures of time, and he knew how to employ and enjoy that possession. The studies by which he gradually digested his mass of reading into principles and convictions exhibit astonishing industry and versatility. They are of all classes, from a chance thought scrawled on the fragment of a letter, to the exhaustive estimate of a standard book or a disputed era. The patient analysis and protracted reflection from which conviction is born are mirrored in manuscripts many times revised. Systems of government, theories of philosophy, the habits and language of the people, the ballads and sayings popular among them, all pass in

c

review in this process of self-education. The future poet was unconsciously nourishing his imagination, the future statesman collecting his data and framing his policy.

The stages by which Davis came to love all he had been taught in childhood to deride or detest can only be a subject of conjecture, but from the earliest record of his opinions by his own hand, they are those of a confirmed Nationalist. He had silently grown into a patriot. This result was not so unexampled as the process by which it was attained. Some of the most conspicuous figures in Irish history, between the fall of Limerick and the emancipation of the Catholics are men who broke away from the party of Protestant ascendancy, and almost the first English writer who recognized the essentially sordid character of Irish Toryism was John Sterling, the grandson of an Irish parson, and the son of a captain of yeomanry. But to most of them their new opinions came from contact with stronger minds; Davis evolved his in the solitude of his college cell.

To complete Maddyn's survey of this early period two or three facts must be mentioned. In 1836, Davis took his degree of B.A., and in the following year was called to the Bar.* In this era he made

---

* The entry in the college books specifies that he "entered 4 July, 1831, as a pensioner; by religion, Protestant; father's

one of those premature and false starts in life which ardent young spirits rarely escape, and which have produced a crop of books the writers would willingly let die, and of speeches which the mature orator shudders to recall. This was the pamphlet to which Maddyn alludes. He had close personal friends among the Dublin Whigs, a party whose policy was leavened at the moment by the generous aims of Hudson, Deasy, O'Hagan, and others, who were afterwards Federalists or Nationalists, and rendered practical by the sympathy of officials of a new type, like Lord Morpeth and Thomas Drummond, then Chief and Under Secretary in Ireland. The House of Lords was at that time making itself odious to reasonable men, by resisting the reform of the Irish Church and Irish Corporations—two of the most indefensible of human institutions; and he made his first plunge into politics before he was quite three and twenty by a plan for the reform of the intractable chamber. It is the argument of a young philosophical Radical for an elected Upper House in the interest of the Empire, and did not differ essen-

---

name, James : profession, a doctor. The boy's age, 16 ; born in County Cork. Educated by Mr. Mongan. Entered under Mr. Luby as college tutor." Mr. Luby, who afterwards was a Fellow, was uncle of Thomas Clarke Luby, a Nationalist of the generation succeeding Davis's, reared on the writings of the Young Irelanders.

tially from the more generous Whig opinions of the time. It is the only work of his hands of which it may be said that the style is tame, and the tone unpersuasive. But it is notable that, even in the storm of political passion which then prevailed, he did not desire to abridge the authority of a second chamber. The absolute power of rejecting bills, he insisted, "should on no account be touched." It was an indispensable check on rash proposals, but it ought to be transferred from irresponsible to responsible hands.*

This pamphlet is the last incident in the era of silent meditation; after his call to the Bar he had a higher call to the true work of his life.

---

* *The Reform of the Lords*, by a Graduate of the Dublin University. Dublin : published for the Author by Messrs. Goodwin & Co., Printers, 29 Denmark Street, 1837. (He still knew so little of the commerce of literature as to adopt a method of publication which rendered a successful sale impossible.)

CHAPTER II.

THE THINKER. 1839, 1840.

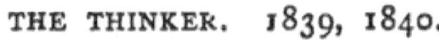

T was not to such a Society as Maddyn describes—gay and sceptical, somewhat sensual and worldly, devoured with ambition for immediate applause, and scarcely more Irish in spirit than if it met by the Isis or the Cam instead of the Liffey —that Davis, in the summer of 1840, delivered his first public address. New men had joined in considerable numbers since the reorganization of 1839, and the Society had become more serious and sincere.

The address was a profound surprise to his few intimate friends, almost as much as to the bulk of the students. Where they expected familiar platitudes on a subject exhausted by use, they heard the voice of an original man, who echoed no one, but uttered his own opinions with the fervour of complete conviction.

The dumb man spoke, and spoke like a mature
teacher.   It was like the fruit of the fig-tree, rich and
succulent, but of which no preliminary blossoms had
given warning.   Wallis, who was present, and who
was among those who expected little, bears witness to
its immediate effect:—

"It excited the surprise and admiration even of those
who knew him best, and won the respect of numbers
who, from political or personal prejudices, had been
originally most unwilling to admit his worth.   So signal
a victory over long-continued neglect and obstinate
prejudice, as he had at length obtained, has never
come under my observation, and I believe it to be unexampled.   There is no assurance of greatness so unmistakable as this.   No power is so overwhelming, no
energy so untiring, no enthusiasm so indomitable as that
which slumbers for years, unconscious and unsuspected,
until the character is completely formed, and then bursts
at once into light and life, when the time for action is
come."

The annual address had commonly consisted of an
éloge on the art of oratory, with individual criticism on
the great masters, and suggestions for the training by
which an orator whom the familiar axiom described
as a manufactured article, might be made.   He rejected this formulary and spoke to the sons of the
gentry and professional classes, of the duties which
would presently await them when they passed from
the college to practical life, and bade them consider
not how to harangue successfully at the Bar or in the

Pulpit, but how they might best become serviceable citizens and good Irishmen.

A *précis* or extracts will give an inadequate impression of this address, but it marks a starting point in his life, and some fragments of it are essential to this narrative.

In joining a society founded for the study of history, he reminded the students that they practically acknowledged how defective was the system of teaching in the University. There they passed the precious time between boyhood and manhood in studying two dead languages imperfectly, and left college loaded with cautions like Swift, or with honours like many a blockhead whom they knew: but ignorant of the events which had happened, the truths which had been discovered, and all that imagination had produced for seventeen hundred years; ignorant of all history, including that of their own country, and for modern literature left to the chances of a circulating library or a taste beyond that of their instructors. Many of the defects of the college system might, he insisted, be remedied by a wise use of the Historical Society. It could teach the things which a student ought to know—primarily the history of his own country—and lay broad and deep the foundations of political knowledge. Three out of four of the orators of the last eighty years (the oratorical period in these king-

doms) were trained, like all the great orators of Greece
and Rome, in such societies.

"'Tis a glorious world, historic memory.   From the
grave the sage warns; from the mound the hero, from
the temple the orator-patriot inspires; and the poet sings
in his shroud.   On the field of fame, the forum of
power, the death-bed or scaffold of the patriots, 'who
died in righteousness'—you look—you pause—you
'swear like them to live, like them to die.'

"With rare exceptions, national history does dramatic
justice to the transactions with which it deals; alien
history is the inspiration of a traitor.   The histories of
a country, by hostile strangers, should be refuted and
then forgotten.   Such are most histories of Ireland; and
yet Irishmen neglect the original documents, and com-
pilations like Carey's 'Vindiciæ;' and they sin not by
omission only—too many of them receive and propagate
on Irish affairs 'quicquid Anglia mendax in historia
audet.'

"The national mind should be filled to overflowing with
native memories.   They are more enriching than mines
of gold, or fields of corn, or the cattle on a thousand
hills; more ennobling than palaced cities stored with the
triumphs of war or art; more supporting in danger's
hour than colonies, or fleets, or armies.   The history of
a nation is the birthright of her sons—who strips them
of that, 'takes that which enricheth not himself but
makes them poor indeed.'"

Not national records alone, but all history taught
great lessons.   Who could discuss the revolutions
which reformed England, convulsed France, and
liberated America, without becoming a wiser man;

who could speculate on their career and not warm with hope?

It was the destiny of most of his audience to enter public life, and he reminded them of its duties and temptations to young Irishmen.

"In your public career you will be solicited by a thousand temptations to sully your souls with the gold and place of a foreign court, or the transient breath of a dishonest popularity; dishonest, when adverse to the good, though flattering to the prejudice, of the people. You will be solicited to become the misleaders of a faction, or the gazehounds of a minister. Be jealous of your virtue; yield not. Bid back the tempter. Do not grasp remorse. Nay, if it be not a vain thought, in such hours of mortal doubt, when the tempted spirit rocks to and fro, pause, and recall one of your youthful evenings, and remember the warning voice of your old companion, who felt as a friend, and used a friend's liberty.

"I do not fear that any of you will be found among Ireland's foes. To her every energy should be consecrated. Were she prosperous, she would have many to serve her, though their hearts were cold in her cause. But it is because her people lie down in misery and rise to suffer, it is therefore you should be more deeply devoted. Your country will, I fear, need all your devotion. She has no foreign friend. Beyond the limits of green Erin there is none to aid her. She may gain by the feuds of the stranger; she cannot hope for his peaceful help, be he distant, be he near; her trust is in her sons. You are Irishmen. She relies on your devotion; she solicits it by her present distraction and misery. I have prayed that I might see the day when, amid the reverence of those, once her foes, her sons would—

'Like the leaves of the shamrock unite,
A partition of sects from one foot-stalk of right :
Give each his full share of the earth and the sky,
Nor fatten the slave where the serpent would die.'

"But not only by her sufferings does Ireland call upon you : her past history furnishes something to awake proud recollections.   I speak not of that remote and mysterious time when the men of Tyre traded to her well-known shores, and every art of peace found a home on her soil ; and her armies, not unused to conquest, traversed Britain and Gaul.   Nor yet of that time when her colleges offered a hospitable asylum to the learned and the learning of every land, and her missions bore knowledge and piety through savage Europe ; nor yet of her gallant and romantic struggles against Dane, and Saxon, and Norman ; still less of her hardy wars, in which her interest was sacrificed to a too-devoted loyalty in many a successful, in many a disastrous battle.   Not of these.   I speak of sixty years ago.   The memory is fresh, the example pure, the success inspiring.   I speak of the 'Lifetime of Ireland.'"

To each age God gave a career of possible improvement.   In their time his young audience could foresee the speedy rise of democracy, and they had it in their power to accelerate and regulate its march.

"A great man has said, if you would qualify the democracy for power you must 'purify their morals, and warm their faith, if that be possible.'* How awful a

* De Tocqueville, preface to *La Démocratie en Amerique.*

doubt! But it is not the morality of laws, nor the religion of sects, that will do this. It is the habit of rejoicing in high aspirations and holy emotions; it is charity in thought, word, and act; it is generous faith, and the practice of self-sacrificing virtue. To educate the heart and strengthen the intellect of man are the means of ennobling him. To strain every nerve to this end, is the duty from which no one aware of it can shrink.

"I speak not of private life—in it our people are tender, generous, and true-hearted. BUT, GENTLEMEN, YOU HAVE A COUNTRY. The people among whom we were born, with whom we live, for whom, if our minds are in health, we have most sympathy, are those over whom we have power—power to make them wise, great, good. Reason points out our native land as the field for our exertion, and tells us that without patriotism a profession of benevolence is the cloak of the selfish man."

Davis did not altogether omit the aids and suggestions for self-education, of which the annual address had ordinarily consisted, and his counsel was of the most precise and practical character, and gives incidentally an insight into the studies by which he made himself a master of English prose.

But he passed speedily from the mere instrumental parts of knowledge to the higher methods by which it is acquired and used.

"Every prudent man will study subjects, not authors. Learning is the baggage of the orator: without it, he may suffer exhaustion or defeat from an inferior foe;

with it, his speed and agility are diminished. Those are best off who have it in magazines, to be drawn on occasion. Learning is necessary to orator, and poet, and statesman. Book-learning, when well digested, and vivified by meditation, may suffice, as in Burke and Coleridge; but otherwise it is apt to produce confusion and inconsistency of mind, as it sometimes did in both these men.

"When Grattan paced his garden, or Burns trod his hillside, were they less students than the print-dizzy denizens of a library? No; that pale form of the Irish regenerator is trembling with the rush of ideas; and the murmuring stream, and the gently rich landscape, and the fresh wind converse with him through keen interpreting senses, and tell mysteries to his expectant soul, and he is as one inspired; arguments in original profusion, illustrations competing for his favour, memories of years long past, in which he had read philosophy, history, poetry, awake at his call. That man entered the senate-house, no written words in his hand, and poured out the seemingly spontaneous, but really learned and prepared lullaby over Ireland's cradle, or keen over Ireland's corse."

These fragments, more than anything which he has left behind, enable us to divine the process by which the young Conservative became a Nationalist. It is plain that he had slowly thought out his opinions, and was sailing by no conventional chart, but by fixed stars.*

When the lecture was printed, the sympathetic

---

*The entire address, which is infinitely worthy of study, may be found in Mr. Rolleston's *Prose Writings of Thomas Davis*.

student naturally sent it to the two or three contemporary thinkers who were the most familiar companions of his solitude. One was Savage Landor, in whose *Imaginary Conversations* he found a storehouse of noble thoughts, though his unbridled temper and rash spirit had left him shorn of the influence his genius might have commanded. Landor's reply was found among Davis's correspondence :—

"Bath, Sunday evening, December 15, 1840.
"Sir,
"I return you many thanks for the honour you have done me, in sending me the Address read before the Historical Society of Dublin.

"I hope it may conduce to the cultivation of the national mind. Ireland, I forsee, will improve more in the next fifty years than any other country in Europe, between steam and Father Mathew.

"That man has done greater good than all the founders of all the religions in the world within an equal space of time. I would rather see your countrymen flock round such leaders than expose their heads to the dangerous flourishes of declamatory demagogues.

"I am, sir,
"Your very obliged and obedient servant,
"W. S. LANDOR."

In John Forster's *Life of Landor* we find Davis's rejoinder, and get a glimpse of the political opinions which were consolidating into convictions. He had no personal relations with O'Connell as yet, but he recognized him as the legitimate successor of the historical Irishmen whose lives were his favourite study.

"I am glad to find you have hopes for Ireland. You have always had a good word and, I am sure, good wishes for her. If you knew Mr. Mathew you would relish his simple and downright manners. He is joyous friendly, and quite unassuming. To have taken away a degrading and impoverishing vice from the hearts and habits of three millions of people in a couple of years seems to justify any praise to Mr. Mathew, and also to justify much hope for the people. And suffer me to say that if you knew the difficulties under which the Irish struggle, and the danger from England and from the Irish oligarchy, you would not regret the power of the political leaders, or rather Leader, here; you would forgive the exciting speeches, and perchance sympathize with the exertions of men who think that a domestic Government can alone unite and animate all our people. Surely the desire of nationality is not ungenerous, nor is it strange in the Irish (looking to their history); nor considering the population of Ireland, and the nature and situation of their home, is the expectation of it very wild."

He wrote also to Wordsworth, and received a friendly answer; but this correspondence has been lost.*

---

* Davis told John O'Hagan that Wordsworth praised the address as a composition and as regards many of the sentiments, but said that it contained "too much insular patriotism." The pamphlet was dedicated to the memory of Francis Kearney, one of his early associates, who was now dead.

The powers of the secluded student were now confessed, and when he found wings it was as natural for
Davis to use them as for a young bird to fly. The
Citizen was under the management of his friends
McCullagh and Wallis, and the studies which had
occupied his long leisure in college were poured without stint into that barren soil. A youth of constant
study, a manhood in which he pondered over principles
and systems, prepared him to speak with authority on
many questions. It is a strangely touching experiment to turn over these papers to-day, and mark the
care he bestowed upon subjects of the profoundest
national importance, but to which scarcely any one
else gave a thought. *Udalism and Feudalism* is
a contrast of Norway and Ireland—the one solidly prosperous with a peasant proprietary, the other starving
and desperate with a tenantry at will. In the same
spirit he investigated the constitutional difficulties
which arose in the time of Grattan ; and in a paper on
the natural relation of Irishmen to the Afghans (then
defending their liberties), opened up views of a foreign
policy suitable to a people in the position of the Irish,
which were afterwards reiterated in the *Nation*, and
which a thousand later echoes have rendered commonplace, and at times *outré* and extravagant. But the
most solid and valuable of these studies was a later
inquiry into the work done by the maligned Irish Par-

liament of James II.   These essays would have helped
to train a generation in the knowledge that makes good
citizens; but the public mind was still cold and indifferent.   In truth, the Celtic temperament is averse
to abstract studies, and will only bend to them under
strict discipline, or when they have become the fuel of
a great passion.

The friends with whom Davis was in the most affectionate and confidential relation at this time, outside
the *Citizen* circle, were John Blake Dillon, William
Eliot Hudson, and Robert Patrick Webb.   Dillon
was a fellow-student of his own age and character,
whom he had encountered at the Historical Society—

"A simple, loyal nature, pure as snow."

Webb was a school-fellow at Mr. Mongan's seminary,
and a constant associate from early days; a young
man of leisure, culture, and liberal tastes, and, though
of Conservative training and associations, disposed
to follow his friend into new fields.   Hudson was
several years the senior of Davis; a man of sweet,
serene disposition, and singularly unselfish patriotism.
He held the office of Taxing Master in the Four Courts,
and had been associated with O'Loghlen Perrin and
the leading Whig lawyers in reforming the administration of justice in Ireland.   But his leisure and income
were devoted to projects of public usefulness, in which
ambition had no share, for his name was never heard

outside of his own circle. National airs were collected and published at his cost, and various studies in Celtic literature promoted, and he bore the burthen of the *Citizen*, which was published at a constant loss, and contributed from time to time valuable papers in the region of political science. The maxim which declares that "a man may be known by his friends" was very applicable to Davis's case; it is only round such a man that such friends cluster.

CHAPTER III.

THE POLITICIAN.   1841, 1842.

T was in the spring of 1841, early in his twenty-fifth year, that Davis passed from speculation to action, and for the first time took a personal part in promoting the broad national policy which he had advocated in the *Citizen*. In the previous autumn the Whigs had committed a wanton outrage on the feelings of Irish gentlemen. To provide a conspicuous office for a few weeks for a political gladiator of their following,* who had grown discontented, they compelled the greatest orator whom Ireland had sent to their aid since Edmund Burke to retire from the Irish Chancellorship, and placed a Scotch lawyer of hard and vulgar nature at the

---

* Sir John Campbell, afterwards Lord Campbell.

head of the Irish bar. Davis attended a bar-meeting
of remonstrance, chiefly Whigs of national opinions
who resented the appointment, not as a question
of professional etiquette, but because it tended to
humiliate Ireland. But the remonstrance caused
scarcely a ripple of opinion. The middle class had
tasted patronage and fallen asleep at the feet of the
Whigs, and as O'Connell, who detested Plunket, was
silent, the mass of the people did not know that there
was anything amiss.*

It was in company with Conservatives resisting
another Whig offence that Davis entered on the stage
to do something which attracted universal attention,
because it was something which no other Liberal in
Ireland of that day would have attempted.

The Royal Dublin Society was an institution created
by the Irish Parliament for promoting the useful arts
and sciences, and developing the natural resources of
the country. After the Union, Leinster House, the
palace of the Geraldines, was purchased for its use,
and it received an annual grant of £5,500 to defray

---

* O'Connell is said to have approved of the transaction. It is
manifest from his private correspondence that he did not share
the professional or political heat on the subject. " Blessed be
God, the danger is over ! [defeat of the Government]. I believe
Lord Plunket is about to resign. Campbell will be his successor." (O'Connell to P. V. Fitzpatrick, London, April 29,
1839, *Private Correspondence of O'Connell*, edited by W. J.
Fitzpatrick).

the cost of its museum, schools of design, botanic garden, annual exhibition of cattle and agricultural produce, and occasional exhibitions of native manufactures. The lethargy which fell upon Irish enterprise after the provincialization of Dublin, was peculiarly felt in literary and scientific institutions, and the Dublin Society became less and less a school of practical science and more and more a party club. It maintained a news-room and lending library for its members, with a subscription so high as to be nearly prohibitory to all but the landed gentry. When the era of reform came with the Whigs, its shortcomings fell under the review of Parliament, and in 1836 a select committee reported that, to answer the purpose for which it was endowed, it must be effectually reorganized.

Something was done to carry out the orders of Parliament, but not much. The high subscription was maintained, and it continued so exclusively a party club that the council was taken in a large degree from the party of Protestant ascendancy. Two or three years after Catholic Emancipation a minority, who thought it not too soon to recognize the fact that religious equality among all classes of Irishmen was established by law, proposed Dr. Murray, the Archbishop of Dublin, a member of its council. He was a man who, from the sweetness of his disposition and the moderation of his opinions, had made no personal enemies ; but he was a Catholic and a priest, and the society rejected him by a large majority. There was wide and profound indignation, which the Whig Government, of whom Dr. Murray was an ally, shared, and the transaction naturally brought the general short-comings of the society into view. At the close of 1840, when the estimates for the coming year were in preparation, Lord Morpeth, then Irish Secretary, reminded the society that the House of Commons had recommended certain essential reforms which were not yet effected. He intimated that they must abandon the political news-room, reduce the annual fee, and abolish the lending library on which funds granted for the promotion of science were expended, and carry out more effectually the instructions of Parliament, or the endowment could not be continued. The council, in reply, contended that they had carried out the instructions of Parliament as far as was reasonably practicable ; that the news-room was supported, not out of the endowment, but out of the personal subscriptions of members ; and they insisted that the arbitrary command issued to them was not justified by any solid grounds, and was derogatory to the character of the society as an independent body. A general meeting of the society approved of this answer by a majority of 129 to 57. The Government organ, the

Dublin Evening Post, immediately announced that the parliamentary grant would be withdrawn.*

In the state of public opinion in Ireland at that time, nine-tenths of those who called themselves Reformers, whether Protestants or Catholics, applauded this *coup* of the Government. It was an effectual method of punishing a bigoted coterie, who neglected the duties for which they were responsible and insulted a man of the blameless character of Dr. Murray. But to Davis the question was not one between Catholic and Protestant, or Liberal and Conservative, but between Ireland and the Imperial Government. He was offended by the arbitrary treatment of Irish gentle-men, and probably hoped that they would understand they were insulted because they were Irishmen. He wrote an article, marked by lofty national sentiment and an open contempt for party feeling on such a subject ; and Dillon, who had some acquaintance with the editor of the *Morning Register,* took it to that journal. The readers of the Whig Catholic paper,

---

* An official letter from the Under Secretary confirmed the news. The society was informed that His Excellency could not recommend to Parliament any further continuance of the annual grant. He was, however, ready to receive from the council an account of any liabilities incurred previous to the receipt of Lord Morpeth's letter of the 17th of December, which were " essential to the promotion of the objects of the institution," that he might consider what sum should be introduced into the estimate of the present year for their liquidation.

famous for statistics and habitually deferential to the Castle, must have read next morning with lively surprise an appeal to sentiments of Protestant nationality long forgotten in Irish controversy.*

"Was this the tone to adopt to a great national body? —'You are our pensioners, do just as we bid you, without regard to your own opinions or your own convenience, or we dismiss you.' . . . Was this the treatment due to an institution which had grown old in serving the interests of Ireland? Grant that the society was wrong, yet surely it deserved respect and patience. It deserved more; its opinions should not have been disregarded; its wishes should in some degree have been yielded to. We ask, Would the French Government treat a public institution thus? Would the English treat an English society of old standing, great numbers, and respectability, thus? No, they dare not. Verily, we are provincials. This society has existed over one hundred years; it contains eight hundred members; it maintains a body of professors of arts and sciences; it has schools, theoretical and practical, for teaching; the agriculture, the manufactures, the science, the literature of Ireland, have been served by it; and now it is to be flung aside at the caprice of an English Government. We remember well that the society did, on one remarkable occasion, richly deserve the charge of having acted factiously. A venerated prelate, who united all that endears the man with all that ennobles the public character, was rejected from political, or worse, from sectarian feeling. We were not behind in censuring them; but we deny that there is any connection be-

* Dublin *Morning Register*, Feb. 2, 1841.

tween that step and this; neither the same men nor the same motives have influenced the society now."

The Castle press was bewildered by sentiments so unprecendented. A Liberal journal, complaisant to the Castle, and perhaps under obligations to official persons, resisting the will of the Government! It was unheard of; a base motive was the only one intelligible to the official journalist, and he affirmed that the proprietor of the *Register* must have been betrayed in his absence by some untrustworthy representative.

Mr. Conway—this was the name of the Castle journalist—scoffed at the idea of Tory nationality; but Davis knew that Irish patriotism had been constantly recruited from the ranks of its hereditary enemies. Its greatest spokesmen for a century were sons of Government officials, while in every generation the sons of historical and tribunitial houses had passed over to the enemy, or silently relinquished the opinions which made their ancestors illustrious. He was persuaded that it only needed a Swift or a Grattan to revive the Protestant nationality of old.

Dillon next day restated the grounds on which the society was defended.

The society was saved, and the sympathetic reader may mark that this transaction presents a key-note to Davis's entire career.

The friends felt that they had got an opening to the

mind of the country which ought not to be lightly relinquished, and they resolved to propose a more permanent arrangement to Mr. Staunton. The result was
that the two young men were placed in control of the
Register, for a limited period, and strictly as an experiment. Since a national press existed in Ireland it
was never so low in character and ability as at that
time. The popular journals echoed the speeches of
O'Connell, but rarely supplemented them by any individual thought or investigation. One nowhere encountered the convictions and purpose of an independent man. The journalists at this time worked for
the most part with the lethargy of men who believed
little and hoped nothing. Thomas Moore summed up
the case : " Look," he said, "at the Irish papers. The
country in convulsion—people's lives, fortunes, and
religion at stake, and not a gleam of talent from one
year's end to the other." But though the press was
feeble it was often malicious, like a torpid viper, it
awoke at times to inflict a sting.

National literature in a higher sense than journalism,
like all our native institutions, had emigrated to England.
The poet who, in the eyes of Europe, typified the Irish
race vegetated in Devonshire. The novelist who
aimed to win for the annals of Scotia Major the interest
with which Scott had invested the annals of Scotia
Minor was fagging for London booksellers. The

young man of genius who had produced the most
original drama of the generation, and a novel which
more than one of his rivals has pronounced to be the
best Irish story ever written, was starving in a London
garret because he could not get even the employment
of a hack. Lady Morgan, after attempting for a time
to sustain a national *salon* in Dublin, followed the tide
and established herself in Mayfair. Maxwell was still
labouring, nearly as unsuccessfully as Maturin had
laboured before him, to attract an audience to pure
literature flavoured with a dash of Irish eccentricity;
and Mag nn and Mahony, both intensely Irish in
nature and gifts, exhibited their nationality chiefly in
bitter gibes at O'Connell and the Repealers. The
Irish Penny Magazine, in which Petrie and O'Donovan
had revived for a time the study of Irish antiquities,
was dead. A *Dublin Penny Journal,* owned by a
Scotch firm, followed, but did not succeed it. The
Citizen was little read, and, except for occasional historical papers, was not worth reading. The *Dublin
University Magazine* alone maintained the reputation
of Irish genius, but it was more habitually libellous of
the Irish people than the *Times.* The stories of
Carleton and LeFanu, the poetry and criticism of
Mangan and Anster, the graphic sketches of Cæsar
Otway, and the sympathetic essays of Samuel Ferguson
were smothered in masses of furious bigotry manu-

factured chiefly by Samuel O'Sullivan, a parson who had once been a papist, and brought to his new connection the zeal of a convertite. His brother, Mortimer O'Sullivan, a man of notable ability, was also a contributor, but rarely fell into the monotony of hysterics which distinguished his junior. The voice of Irish Ireland was heard nowhere but in the speeches of O'Connell, and his position and antecedents made him less the national than the Catholic champion.

The young men wrote constantly in the *Register* on foreign politics, and national organization; and, for the first time since the corpse of Robert Emmet was flung into the mud of Bullysacre, a perfectly genuine appeal was made to Protestant nationality. The first fate of new truths is to be ridiculed, and the country was then in no humour to be schooled in the sterner virtues. Corrupted by the Whigs, who had kindled the lust of place in a million of hearts—from the popular member who wanted a sinecure, to the young peasant who wanted to be a policeman,—the new principles made no way. The ordinary clientele of the *Register* did not understand them; and to gather new readers around a long-established paper, with a fixed reputation for respectable mediocrity, was a disheartening and nearly impossible task. The prejudice to be assailed was peculiarly intractable. Irish Protestants might well be ashamed of the wrongs they permitted and battened upon, but most of them only saw their country through a haze of traditional prejudice. A pane of coloured glass alters the eternal facts of nature, her grass is no longer green or her skies blue, and their prejudice was a coloured glass through which all nature looked orange and purple. The experiment was to last for three months certain, and then be reconsidered. Mr. Staunton, who was hard and parsimonious, but strictly honest in business transactions, reported, when the time came, that it had not succeeded. In July he wrote to Davis.

" MY DEAR SIR,

"Our agreement was made on the 5th of March, and, according to my reckoning, you were engaged sixteen weeks subsequently to that date. You are therefore entitled to £32, for which I enclose a draft. There is, I am sorry to say, no dividend to be computed, our condition having been the opposite of one in advance.

"Yours very truly,

"MICH. STAUNTON.*

"Thomas Davis, Esq."

We constantly expect from a gifted man qualities which he does not possess. Davis was a great journalist ; he might have become a great orator ; he did, after a little, become a great poet ; but he never exhibited the practical faculty which makes circumstances

* 80 Marlborough Street, July 24th.

its submissive agents. The *Citizen*, into which he poured the treasures of his mind, attracted no national interest ; and the *Register*, while he poured political philosophy and national spirit into its leading columns, was, from title-page to tail-piece, merely a respectable Government utensil. The men in Ireland at that era who possessed the practical faculty in the greatest perfection were O'Connell and Thomas Drummond, but both of them wanted some of Davis's higher spiritual gifts.

The two friends immediately retired from the *Register*, and employed themselves in other public work. They had found work by this time, destined to engross the remainder of their lives. While writing in the *Register* it became plain that their position as national journalists, standing outside of the national organization which O'Connell had recently re-established at the Corn Exchange, was weak and anomalous. The philosophical nationality of the University was a feeble fire at best, and it was certain that it would only spread slowly and probably not very far. On the other hand, the popular agitation naturally repelled a young man like Davis, bred among a class to whom it was hateful and contemptible. For its methods were of necessity coarse, its instruments rude, and the one conspicuous man of genius who gave it its sole authority was the living embodiment of political and religious passions inherited from former contests. But, however imperfectly it fulfilled its office, it was the only guardian of the national cause, and that cause was the cause of justice. The result of reflection was that, to accomplish his purpose, he must do what Tone had done before him—he must associate himself with the Catholic people and their trusted leaders. The most courageous incident in Davis's career, which would not have been surpassed in daring if he had mounted a breach in promotion of his opinions, was to enter the Corn Exchange and announce himself a follower of Daniel O'Connell.

It is difficult at the close of the nineteenth century, after fifty years of agitation for national ends in which Protestants have been leaders or conspicuous spokesmen, to understand what such a decision meant in 1842. The son of a Roman centurion who left the retinue of Cæsar to associate with the obscure Hebrews gathered round Saul of Tarsus scarcely made a more surprising or significant choice. A dozen years had barely elapsed since the Celtic population were released from a code expressly framed for their extinction, so that "one Papist should not remain in Ireland." The bulk of the nation were simple, generous, and pious, but ignorant, and little accustomed to think for themselves. The middle-class Catholics scarcely dreamed of any higher aim than to obtain some social recognition from the dominant race, or some crumb of patronage from a friendly Administration.

We have glanced at the Ireland into which Davis was born in 1814. The generation which had since elapsed saw political changes accomplished of great scope and promise—Catholics were emancipated and Parliament was reformed,—but the system on which Ireland was governed by England had undergone no substantial change. Every institution and agency pertaining to authority was still strictly Protestant. The towns were only a few months liberated from exclusive corporations who had vindicated their right to govern by plundering in every instance the endowments provided by the State for their support. The counties were controlled (as they are still controlled) by Protestant grand juries, in whose selection the ratepayers whose money they expended had no part. The judiciary, executive, and local magistracy were Protestant in the proportion of more than a hundred to one, and they commonly regarded the people with distrust and aversion ; for though time had mitigated, it had not extinguished the sentiment which in official circles classified the bulk of the nation as the " Irish enemy." Half the rural population were steeped in habitual misery. The peasantry in the genial climate of southern Europe were better clad and fenced against the elements than the tenant farmers who toiled under

the moist and chilly sky of winter in Ireland ; and in
the least productive countries in Europe, in the
barrenest canton of Switzerland, or the most sterile
commune in the Alps, they were better fed than
amongst the plentiful harvests of Munster. The great
estates were held by English absentees, who ruled the
country from Westminster, mainly for their own profit
and security. The resident gentry were for the most
part their dependents or adherents, and had never
wholly lost the secret apprehension that estates obtained by confiscation might in the end be forfeited by
the same process. But they were entrenched behind
a standing army whose function in Dublin was no
more in doubt than that of the Croat in Milan or the
Cossack in Warsaw. The country sent a few national
and a few Catholic representatives to the Imperial
Parliament, but the franchise was so skilfully adjusted
to exclude the majority that in Dublin a citizen with
the required qualification had sometimes to pay as
many as ten separate rates and taxes before he became
entitled to vote. The one powerful tribune, indeed,
constantly demanded in Parliament and on the popular
platform the rights withheld from the people ; but his
enemies scornfully declared that he did not represent
the nation, but only its frieze coats and soutanes. He
had against him, for the most part, the Irishmen whose
books were read or whose lives were notable, the

journalists capable of controlling public opinion, and, universally, the great social power called good society. His agitation was pronounced to be plebeian ; and, in truth, it was not free from faults of exaggeration, offensive to veracity and good taste. For nearly two years O'Connell, at this time, had been making weekly appeals to public opinion in favour of a native Parliament, but he had not drawn to his side one man of station, weight of character, or conspicuous ability. The sincerity of his policy was doubted even among the patriot party, because he impaired the simple force of the national claim by coupling with it a radical reform of the House of Commons, revision of the land code, and the abolition of tithe,—questions to be dealt with by the Imperial Parliament, and each "good for a Trojan war of agitation."

Between the agitator and the Government there stood a section of the Protestant middle-class, of humane culture and liberal opinions, who sympathised with neither, unless when the administration was in the hands of Whigs. They had been Emancipators, and wished to see gross wrongs redressed ; but they were content that reforms should come as soon, and extend as far, as English opinion might approve—unhappily never very soon or very far. They were, in fact, merely the provincial allies of a political party in London.

E

The Tories, who were in a great majority among the gentry and the professions, looked on the popular movement with disdain. But the indolence and satiety which come of long possession leavened their scorn largely with a languid contempt. Between these parties Davis, if he took any part in public affairs, felt he had no choice. He recognized in O'Connell the natural successor of Hugh O'Neil, Art MacMurragh, Owen Roe, and the other Celtic soldiers who had stood in the front of the nation in peril and calamity. No one saw more clearly that the leader was not free from faults—it is only in poetry and romance that one encounters blameless heroes ; but his cause was the same as theirs, the deliverance of the Irish race from greedy and truculent oppression. Among the class whom Davis burned to enlist in the national movement, O'Connell had never stood so low as at this time. He had laid himself open to a suspicion hostile to his influence among men of public spirit. Little more than half a dozen years earlier he had pulled down the banner of nationality, in order to grasp the patronage of the Irish Government, and they believed that if the Whigs came back to power he would yield again to the same temptation. He could doubtless plead in defence that he had brought into power the Irish administration of Mulgrave and Drummond, and raised O'Loghlen and Woulfe to the bench.

In 1840 the Government which he supported fell from power, and he immediately took up the national question anew.

But he was impeded at every step by inevitable suspicions; the majority of the nation answered languidly to his appeal, and the minority did not answer at all.

This was a country in which a public career offered no prizes to ambition, but nowhere on the earth was a noble, unselfish patriotism more imperiously solicited to struggle and die rather than endure wrongs so shameless. The patriotism of the two young men was not solicited in vain; on the 19th of April, 1841, Davis and Dillon became members of the Repeal Association. They were cordially welcomed by O'Connell, and immediately placed on the General Committee, which was the popular privy council, and on sub-committees charged with special duties. How they demeaned themselves there I shall describe more conveniently a little later, when I became their associate.

They were assiduous in their attendance on committees, but they did not limit their labours for the national cause to one field. Davis continued his contributions to the *Citizen*—now become the *Dublin Monthly Magazine;* and Dillon, who had succeeded to the auditorship of the Historical Society, prepared the closing address for the year 1841.

Dillon's address followed the general line of his friend's in teaching public duties, rather than rules of art; but it was calmer and statelier in tone. Nearly devoid of ornament, it was eloquent with strong convictions and lucid principles. It was an appeal to the judgment and conscience rather than to the generous emotions. But it was persuasive in a singular degree. One of the most eminent judges in Ireland* told me a fact which enables us to estimate its value better than much criticism. "The night before I read Dillon's address," he said, "I was a Whig ; next morning and ever after I was a Nationalist." Dillon was so closely associated with Davis, so intimate a confederate and counsellor throughout his career, that I must pause for a moment on the Catholic Nationalist's first confession of faith as an essential part of the new opinions which they brought into Irish affairs.

If the Historical Society were solely a school of eloquence (he told them) the greatest lesson it could teach was that the way to be eloquent was, not to study the tricks of rhetoric, but to cultivate the passions of which eloquence is the natural language. It was usual on occasions like that to praise the care and perseverance of Demosthenes in mastering the art, but it would be more to the purpose to recall "the great

* The late Judge O'Hagan.

passions by which he was inspired ; the ardent love he bore his country ; his fear for her safety ; his undying hatred of her foe ; and his fierce indignation against the traitors to her cause."

And history everywhere repeated the same lesson.

" Look," he said, " to the records of any nation, and inquire what is that period of its history when eloquence shone forth in the greatest splendour? You will find it to be, when great events were being enacted, and great interests in conflict, and great and stormy passions roused in the breasts of men. Compare France in the Revolution with France ten years before, and ask the cause of the change which that short period brought about in the genius of its people? You will find that it was not because they were more accomplished rhetoricians, that the men of the Revolution were greater orators than those who went before them, but because of the bursting forth of new passions, and the diffusion from breast to breast of high and fierce desires. And when Henry, the Demosthenes of America, issued from the recesses of the forest, and summoned his countrymen to arms, with an eloquence as deep, and as strong, and as rapid, as the rivers of his native wild, whence did HE draw his inspiration? Was it from the pages of Longinus, or Quinctilian, or Blair? or was it not rather from the tumultuous emotions that heaved within him? He loved his country ; he saw it in danger ; and passion touched his heart, and its fountains opened, and the sacred stream gushed forth unsolicited and free."

He spoke of the examples which our own history furnish ; and drew from them lessons new to his audience, but which time has made our common property.

" We are apt, when we contemplate such a rare colle-
tion of great men as the Irish Parliament at that time
exhibited, to attribute to THEM the greatness of those
events which occurred in their time. I would be inclined to reverse this arrangement, and to place the
greatness of the time the first, and the greatness of
the men the second, in the order of causation Great
orators they were, no doubt—amongst the greatest the
world ever saw ; but I do not think they deserve to
be classed amongst the greatest men. As men, their
greatness should be judged, not from what they SAID,
but what they DID ; and, judged by this test, they are
found wanting. Their language abounds in great con-
ceptions ; but in their actions we seek in vain for that
lofty determination which marks the conduct of the
truly great—the Hampdens, the Washingtons, and many
a countryman of our own, whose name is now forgotten,
or preserved by lying history as an object of ridicule
and scorn. At a time when they had the enemy completely at their mercy, and might have dictated whatever terms they pleased, they should have insisted on
something more than permission to meet and amuse one
another with elaborate orations, and to make laws which
they had no power to enforce."

He warned them against the modern cosmopoli-
tanism which taught that nationality was a prejudice;
that one spot on earth, because we chanced to be born
there, was not on that account to be preferred to
another, and that we had no duties to perform to our
mother country. The ravages of pestilence and
famine were soon repaired, and fields laid waste soon
grew green again ; but when cold and grovelling

selfishness took possession of the minds of a people and drew them away from virtue and honour, there was then a wound inflicted which festered at the heart, and which centuries might not heal.

He spoke of the blessings patriotism conferred, and the sacrifices it entailed, and it lends a noble charm to the sentiment of the young man to remember that in later times when called upon to put the sentiment into action he did not fail.

Students familiar with the ante-revolution literature of France and America will note that Davis's address belonged to the first, Dillon's to the second school. The one suggests the passion of Vergniaud, the other the stately strength of Patrick Henry or the serene philosophy of Alexander Hamilton. Davis's address was like a vivid stream rippling musically over impediments, and leaping into cascades, sometimes sparkling in the sun, sometimes diving into subterranean places, and reappearing coloured with the veined soil through which it forced its way. Dillon's was like a calm, strong level river, whose force may be measured by the unbroken rapidity of its course.

The adhesion of Davis and Dillon to the popular movement is a memorable event to Irishmen. There are men who make epochs in our history. Lorian O'Thuail, who combined the Celtic tribes against the invader; Art McMurrough, who effaced the crimes

of his ancestors by heroic services ; Hugh O'Neill, who
baffled the enemy by culture and policy, learned in
their own camp and court; Roger O'Moore, who
evoked hope among a moribund people ; Sarsfield,
who restored to their imagination the figure of a
national soldier ; Grattan, who used the institutions
of the conquerors to conquer them in turn ; Wolfe
Tone, who combined the Presbyterian Republicans
of the North with the Catholic serfs of Munster ;
O'Connell, who taught the trampled multitude their
own strength ; and Davis, who once again aimed to
unite the whole force of the nation in honourable
union, are such men.   He was the first Protestant
since Tone who not only sympathized with the wrongs
of the Celts, but accepted and embraced the whole
volume of their hopes and sympathies.   He was not
a patron of the old race, but its spokesman and
brother.

It was at this time, in the autumn of 1841, that I
made Davis's acquaintance at the Repeal Association,
and Dillon's at the *Register* office, where I had preceded him in an apprenticeship to journalism.   I was
in town only for a few days, to keep terms as a law
student, and had no opportunity of cultivating their
acquaintance before returning to Belfast, where I then
edited a bi-weekly newspaper.   But they were so
unlike all I had previously seen of Irish journalists

that I was eager to know more of them. On returning to Dublin in the spring of 1842, I met them in
the hall of the Four Courts, and they put off their
gowns and walked out with me to the Phœnix Park,
to have a frank talk about Irish affairs. We soon
found that our purpose was the same—to raise up
Ireland morally, socially, and politically, and put the
sceptre of self-government into her hands. I knew
their connection with the *Register* had ceased, and
that the *Citizen* had no audience or influence in the
country, and I proposed that we should establish and
conduct a weekly paper as organ of the opinions we
held in common. Sitting under a noble elm in the
park, facing Kilmainham, we debated the project,
and agreed on the general plan. I was to find the
funds and undertake the editorship, and we were to
recruit contributors among our friends. Davis could
count upon John Cornelius O'Callaghan, whose
Green Book * was attracting attention at that
time; Dillon named two young men in College,
who afterwards did valuable work—John O'Hagan
and John Pigot; and I could promise for Clarence

---

* In 1841 appeared *The Green Book; or, Gleanings from
the Writing Desk of a Literary Agitator :* " a miscellany of
poetry ; the notes, valuable historical studies ; the verses, rather
slipshod, being more than ten years older than the establishment
of the *Nation,* and belonging to quite a different school.

Mangan and T. M. Hughes,* who both contributed to
the provincial journal I was then editing, and O'Neill
Daunt (formerly O'Connell's private secretary), whom
I had sounded on the subject. We separated on an
agreement to meet again in summer, and launch the
journal in autumn.

Davis's correspondence during his early connection with the Repeal Association exhibits him constantly engrossed in work.

"I am a brute (he wrote to his friend P. R. Webb)
for not having written to you before. After that admis-
sion you must forgive me. I envy you your leisure, and
your country, and your thoughts. I am up to the tips
of my hair in business. I am secretary to the Franchise
Committee, ditto to the Municipal Election Committee,
and, on account of Clement's illness, I am obliged to
give some of my time to the Dublin Registry, which is
now going on. There is no hope of my getting out of
this 'decayed metropolis' for the summer, or autumn
either"

"Are you getting more passionately patriotic? You
are away from poor Ireland. Poor, poor Ireland! Well,
who knows? 'Old Erin SHALL be free,' says the 'Shan
Van Vocht.' Have you made as much way in De
Beaumont as in walking? [Davis gave him De Beaumont's 'Irlande Sociale, Politique, et Religieuse' to
study.] "

"O'Callaghan is in London, staggering with Parisian

---

* Afterwards author of *Revelations of Spain*, the *Ocean
Flower*, etc., and editor of the *London Charivari* a periodical
which preceded *Punch*, and was illustrated by Leech.

lore. His book is beginning to sell, and will be noticed in the DUBLIN REVIEW next month. Do you know Mackintosh's letters to R. Hall about his madness? Do you know Mackintosh's life? or anything? I only just read it myself, but I can swagger judiciously."*

"You will be glad to hear that O'Connell will (he says) have a book on Irish History from 1172 to 1612 (when the Irish were made not-outlaws) published in October. It will consist of some thirty pages of text, and seven or eight hundred of notes and illustrations, including most of Carey's book to that date. [Carey's "Vindicæ Hibernicæ," a defence of the Irish rising of 1641.] O'Connell's name will get all these collections read, and the memory of Ireland will be enlarged. We may all take advantage of this beginning, and put thoughts into the mind of the country. By heavens, 'tis maddening to see the land without arts or arms, literature or wealth! I am for the sharp remedies. Do you feel any necessity for a creed to satisfy your feelings? Unless one has something of the sort he is apt to grow inactive and uncomfortable. A strong mind must preach or govern or love, a mission or occupation, or a paradise. I must choose between the two first, but I waver and grow sensual and misty (for mine is not a strong mind), so shall probably end in doing neither."†

After our general design for the new journal was settled, Davis proposed modifications to which his colleagues could not cordially assent. He feared that a weekly paper spoke too seldom to be an effective teacher. The *Evening Freeman*, an un-

* 61 Bagot Street, September 28, 1841.
† 61 Bagot Street, Sunday, August 15, 1841.

prosperous offshot of the morning paper which appeared twice a week, was understood to be in the market, and he suggested that we should farm it for a fixed period, and be heard twice a week instead of once. I was unwilling to make this experiment, a weekly journal was my ideal. One of my first purchases with money of my own earning had been a set of the *Examiner* in the time of Hazlitt and the Hunts. A paper like the *Examiner* in its best days, —different in form as well as in spirit from the existing weeklies, original instead of a reprint, and literary quite as much as political—seemed to me the fit medium for criticism and speculation. After much debate it was suggested, probably by Dillon, that we might try both projects simultaneously. Happily the division of forces which the double task would have imposed was avoided by the refusal of the *Freeman* proprietary to accept the arrangement. They shortly afterwards purchased the *Morning Register*, in which Davis and Dillon had recently written, amalgamated it with their daily paper, and the unprofitable *Evening Freeman* slipped quietly out of existence.

But Davis had not yet reconciled himself to the limitations of a weekly paper. And his college friends, Wallis especially, were angrily opposed to any political journal, which, they insisted, must fall under the dictatorship of O'Connell, and lose all initiative and independence. The *Dublin Monthly Magazine*, (so the *Citizen* was now named) if it were only strengthened by the men and money about to be wasted on a weekly paper, would, they contended, do the work designed more effectually—the work being, to create a sounder and more generous opinion on all branches of the Irish question, and cultivate the sympathy of Protestants. On the other hand, if its best men were diverted to other projects, the only organ of high nationality in the country must perish.

Objections to a periodical, because it only appeared once a month, were futile; was there not a periodical in Edinburgh, which appeared only once a quarter, which had saved the fortunes of the Whig party, and won the mind of England to Reform? If such things could be done in Edinburgh, why not in Dublin? These were the arguments pressed upon Davis, especially by Wallis, whom he was accustomed to hear with deference.

When the plan was submitted to me I declined to waste an hour or a shilling on the *Citizen* which was moribund, kept from perishing only by the generosity of Hudson. It would be a fatal blunder to put our new wine into this damaged vehicle. A weekly paper would reach classes who never opened a magazine or review. And there was no reason why its teaching should not be as original and effective as if it were issued only once a month. At any rate after the length we had gone retreat was impossible ; the new paper must be published *coûte que coûte*. Davis agreed that retreat was impossible, but he asked me to consider whether the amount of assistance he could give me under the circumstances would be worth retaining. When he asked the advice of Dillon, then in the country, his vigorous good sense rejected the project as peremptorily as I had done.

"DEAR DAVIS (he wrote)—Although I received your letter two days since it was quite impossible for me to answer it sooner. I have been unable to do anything, or even to think of anything since I came to the country from the state of perpetual motion in which I have been kept. In compliance with your request for a categorical answer to your proposal, I say 'No.' I need hardly tell you that nothing would give me greater pleasure than to make one of those of whom your club will consist, if you succeed in establishing it; but with my present opinions regarding its principal object, it would argue a great want of common prudence in me to join it.

"You must not understand me to mean that it is not desirable that the CITIZEN should flourish. I have not as you are aware, so high an opinion of the utility of a monthly periodical for this country as others have ; but, at the same time, I think it would be by no means without use if it could succeed. But is your project likely to insure it success? I see no reason to think so. It is now two or three years in existence, and it is still a losing speculation ; and what chance is there that it will not be the same to the end of the next three years ? What advantage will it have that it has not had ? I cannot see any, and I think it a pity that the energies of the best men in the country should be wasted in an occupation neither profitable to themselves nor to anyone else ; for you know a magazine which does not pay is not read. Under these circumstances, if you engage in the undertaking, I must be content with wishing you success.

"As to the prospectus [of the NATION], it was my intention (and unfortunately, like most of my intentions, it still remains unfulfilled) to write one, and to send it with yours to Duffy. This is the reason why I have kept yours so long. I do not altogether approve of the one you wrote. It contains many good passages ; but, as a whole, I think it would not answer the purpose for which it was intended. I have taken a copy for Duffy, which I will send him immediately. The original I send back to yourself, as you might wish to improve it. It would be highly desirable to have a good prospectus, and you have done first-rate things in that way.

"Have you seen Duffy's letter in the VINDICATOR ? It struck me as a first-rate production. A weekly paper conducted by that fellow would be an invaluable acquisition. I should like to hear when you intend to leave town, and how you are succeeding in the club affair.

"Ever yours,

"JOHN DILLON."*

---

* Dillon's letter has no date ; but the letter in the *Vindicator*, to which he alludes as recent, is dated June 23, 1842.

After Dillon's letter, Davis began to speak to his friends of the new journal. He still helped the *Dublin Monthly* with important papers, and urged old contributors to help it, but the project of re-organizing it was silently abandoned.

Early in July he wrote to Maddyn :—

" Webb and I leave for the north on Tuesday next. After seeing the County Down, Belfast and Benburb, we mean to loiter round Antrim cliffs to Derry, and maybe to Donegal; and from either I shall return by the Fermanagh Lakes to Dublin, leaving him to close the autumn in the north with his wife and his little ones—God bless them! Webb is always asking for you, and what can I say? I am going to take another dash at the press, but under better auspices than last time. If you write to me at any time before the 25th, care of C. G. Duffy, Esq., VINDICATOR Office, Belfast, I'll get the letter."

On his northern journey Davis opened his heart to his friend on his policy and hopes.

" The machinery at present working for repeal could never, under circumstances like the present, achieve it ; but circumstances must change. Within ten or fifteen years England must be in peril. Assuming this much, I argue thus. Modern Anglicism—*i.e.*, Utilitarianism, the creed of Russell and Peel, as well as of the Radicals —this thing, call it Yankeeism or Englishism, which measures prosperity by exchangeable value, measures duty by gain, and limits desire to clothes, food, and respectability—this damned thing has come into Ireland under the Whigs, and is equally the favourite of the

'Peel' Tories. It is believed in the political assemblies in our cities, preached from our pulpits (always Utilitarian or persecuting); it is the very Apostles' Creed of the professions, and threatens to corrupt the lower classes, who are still faithful and romantic. To use every literary and political engine against this seems to me the first duty of an Irish patriot who can foresee consequences. Believe me, this is a greater though not so obvious a danger as Papal supremacy. So much worse do I think it, that, sooner than suffer the iron gates of that filthy dungeon to close on us, I would submit to the certainty of a Papal supremacy, knowing that the latter should end in some twenty years—leaving the people mad, it might be, but not sensual and mean. Much more willingly would I take the chance of a Papal supremacy, which even a few of us laymen could check, shake, and prepare (if not effect) the ruin of. Still more willingly would I (if Anglicanism, *i.e.*, Sensualism, were the alternative) take the hazard of open war, sure that if we succeeded the military leaders would compel the bigots down, establish a thoroughly national Government, and one whose policy, somewhat arbitrary, would be anti-Anglican and anti-sensual; and if we failed it would be in our power before dying to throw up huge barriers against English vices, and, dying, to leave example and a religion to the next age."

In July, Davis visited me at Belfast, and all the preliminaries were settled for the issue of our prospectus. Davis's draft was adopted with a single amendment, and an addition which I considered of the highest practical importance; the names of the intending contributors were to be published as a guarantee of good faith and personal responsibility.

F

Davis suggested the significant title of the *Nation* for the new paper, and a sentence from the prospectus will indicate our specific aim :—

"Nationality is their first great object—a Nationality which will not only raise our people from their poverty, by securing to them the blessings of a DOMESTIC LEGISLATURE, but inflame and purify them with a lofty and heroic love of country—a Nationality of the spirit as well as the letter—a Nationality which may come to be stamped upon our manners, and literature, and our deeds—a nationality which may embrace Protestant, Catholic, and Dissenter—Milesian and Cromwellian— the Irishman of a hundred generations and the stranger who is within our gates;—not a Nationality which would prelude civil war, but which would establish internal union and external independence; a Nationality which would be recognised by the world, and sanctified by wisdom, virtue, and prudence."

The Belfast of the United Irishmen and the Volunteers, which still claimed to be the chief seat of liberality and letters in the island, had a strong fascination for Davis, but I warned him that he would find the "Athens of Ireland" as ugly and sordid as Manchester; its temples hideous Little Bethels, where Pentilic marble was replaced by unwholesome bricks from the mud of the Lagan, its orators noisy fanatics, and the old historic spirit soured into bigotry worthy of Rochelle, the Belfast of France. To my northern friends Davis was a new and puzzling phenomenon. The Belfast Whigs were Protestant

Liberals, in general sympathy with the English Whigs, but a genuine Nationalist was nearly unknown among them. The Catholic Bishop and clergy to whom I presented my friend saw for the first time an Irish Protestant who recognized the old race as the natural spokesmen of public opinion, who sympathized passionately with the historic memories of which they were proud, but never forgot or permitted others to forget that the Protestant minority were equally Irishmen, however party politics might have separated them from their brethren.

Though his apprenticeship ended and his public life began when he entered the Repeal Association, it was only in the new journal Davis was free to utter his whole mind and able to make himself heard by the nation. His public life lasted barely five years, and seldom in the history of a people have five years been more fruitful of beneficent changes in opinion and action. The story I have to tell is not so much the career of a gifted man as the development of a new era. It is more than half a century since he entered the Corn Exchange; it is over eight and forty years since he was buried at Mount Jerome; and during all this interval the opinions which he taught have been widening their scope, and his name growing dearer to his countrymen. He influenced profoundly the mind of his own generation, and it is not too soon to affirm that he has made a permanent change in the convictions of the nation which he served.

From this date all the incidents of his career are familiar to a hundred witnesses, and pass before us like a panorama.

CHAPTER IV.

THE JOURNALIST. 1842.

HE new journal was announced to appear on the 8th of October, 1842. Davis had only undertaken to write one article a week, and he arrived in town from his northern excursion on the eve of publication.* But he speedily came to see that he had found the true business of his life, and he entered on it with all the decision and energy of his nature. The public were on the alert for the appearance of the *Nation*.

* I found this note among his papers : " I have been expecting you in town for some days. Our first number must make its appearance to-morrow fortnight, and there are many questions to be considered, which will require time and you. Pray come home " (Duffy to Davis, Sept. 23, 1842).

The prospectus and the disclosure of the writers'
names had awakened a certain curiosity, and there
was already at the publishing office a considerable list
of subscribers, and large orders for the first number
from country agents. The two earliest subscribers
were symbolical—men who took slight interest in
current journalism, but much in native literature—the
eminent antiquaries, Eugene Curry and John O'Dono
van. But the existing journalists, as I encountered
them from time to time, warned me, in spite of these
omens, to expect a collapse. We are apt to think of
an eminent man as having been to his contemporaries
all he has become to posterity, but this rarely happens ;
and it will be an encouragement to modest men to
know that it was far from happening to Davis. Since
he began to act in public, he was the subject of contemptuous banter to the veteran agitators around
O'Connell. He spoke a language which they did not
understand, and pursued aims which they believed to
be quixotic. The jolly unprincipled editor of the
Pilot, understood to be much in the confidence of
O'Connell, assured me that Davis was a simpleton
who nearly ruined Alderman Staunton by eccentric
proposals in the *Register*, and might be counted on
to frighten men of sense from any enterprise in which
he was concerned. And the proprietor of the *Monitor*,
who had no *malus animus*, told me that he had seen

Davis representing the Repeal Association in the Dublin Revision Court, and that he was unskilful and unready, ignorant of practice which had become traditional, and incapable of holding his own with the Conservative agent. He might be able to write, but he certainly was not able to act.

On the 15th of October the long-expected first number was issued. Maddyn had suggested a happy motto from a speech of Stephen Woulfe, "To create and foster public opinion, and make it racy of the soil." The form and appearance of the journal were new in Ireland; political verses were printed among the leading articles as claiming equal attention, and there was a distinct department for literature. The first leader declared, as the chief article of our creed, that, political nicknames—Whig, Tory, and so forth notwithstanding,—we would recognize only two parties in Ireland—those who suffered by her degradation, and those who profited by it. Clarence Mangan proclaimed our second purpose to be the emancipation of the trampled tenantry.

" We announce a New Era—be this our first news—
When the serf-grinding landlords shall shake in their
    shoes,
When the ark of a bloodless and mighty Reform
Shall emerge from the flood of the popular storm !
Well we know how the lickspittle panders to pow'r
Feel and fear the approach of that death-dealing hour ;

But we toss these aside—such vile, vagabond lumber
Are but just worth a groan from ‘THE NATION’S
   FIRST NUMBER.’ ”

By a curious coincidence the arrangements were
completed on Davis’s twenty-eighth birthday, and
next morning the journal was flying through the city.
In his correspondence with Maddyn we have the
story of its success.

“ The NATION sold its whole impression of No. 1 before twelve o’clock this morning, and could have sold
twice as many more if they had been printed, as they
ought to have been ; but the fault is on the right side.
The office window was actually broken by the newsmen
in their impatience to get more.   The article called
‘ The Nation ’ is by Duffy ; ‘ Aristocratic Institutions,’
by Dillon ; ‘ Our First Number,’ by Mangan ; ‘ Ancient
Irish Literature,’ ‘ The Epigram on Stanley,’ and the
capital ‘ Exterminators’ Song,’ are by O’Callaghan. The
article on ‘ The English Army in Afghanistan, etc.,’ the
mock proclamation to the Irish soldiers, and the reviews
of the two Dublin magazines, are by myself. . . . The
articles you propose would do admirably in your hands.
Duffy is the very greatest admirer of the sketches of
Brougham and Peel that I ever met.   [Sketches by
Maddyn in the DUBLIN MONTHLY MAGAZINE.] Perhaps
in a newspaper the points should be more salient and
the writing more rough and uncompromising than in
a magazine.   Duffy seems to think that if number three,
your lightest, dare-devilish POTEEN article, were to come
first, it would most readily fall in with the rest of the
arrangements.”

Wallis, who was nothing if not critical, administered a bitter to correct any excess of sweets. He wrote to Davis :

"I have not yet seen the new birth to unrighteousness, the unclean thing, with the holy name embroidered on its frontlets and phylacteries. [He objected vehemently to the title of the journal.] Not a copy procurable by me, and sundry other speculative individuals, even at a premium. One thing you may be sure of : the newsmen are open-mouthed against you. I have listened with pastoral patience to several of their diatribes. They say you might have sold in Dublin TEN TIMES what you printed for the city circulation ; and that they warned you early in the week, and offered to lift you and your compeers to the Seventh Heaven on a pyramid of two hundred quires, and you had not the spunk to venture."*

Maddyn, who had made difficulties at the outset in helping a journal with whose main aim he was not in sympathy, soon became a regular contributor of critical and biographical papers ; and Davis treated him with a frank confidence and affectionate deference which soothed the sensitive literary spirit. He sent him suggestions for articles from time to time, and kept him acquainted with the secret history of the enterprise.

"The paper is selling finely. The authorships this

---

* October 17th.

week run thus—'War with Everybody,' by J. F.
Murray; 'Reduction of Rents,' and the 'Faugh a
Ballagh,' by Duffy; 'Time no Title,' 'The Sketch of
Moore,' and 'The Grave,' by myself. . . . The MAIL
says we are at work to establish a French party!
They'll say by-and-by we have Hoche's ghost or the
National Guard in the back office; but devil may care,
    'Foes of Freedom FAUGH A BALLAGH.''

And again :—

"Duffy and I are delighted at your undertaking the
notice of Father Mathew. In your hands, and with
your feeling, the article will be worthy of the man.
The portrait of him will not be out of Landell's hands
for a little time. The Shiel or the Avonmore and
O'Loghlen would probably come best next. The country
people are delighted with us if their letters speak true.
We have several ballads, ay, and not bad ones, ready;
'Noctes,' 'squibs,' etc., in preparation. In the present
number, 'The Reduction of Rents,' and the 'Conti-
nental Literature,' with the translation from La Men-
nais (who has, I see, turned missionary), are by Dillon.
'The O'Connell Tribute' is by Daunt (aided by Duffy's
revision and my quotation from Burke). 'The Revolution in Canada,' and 'An Irish Vampire,' are mine.

Ballads and songs, founded on incidents of Irish
history, had been a speciality in the Belfast journal
which I edited—Clarence Mangan, Dr. Murray, a professor in Maynooth College, and T. M. Hughes, as
well as the editor, had joined in this experiment—and
I consulted Davis and Dillon on the policy of con-
tinuing them in the *Nation*. Neither of them had

ever published a line of verse, but they were willing
to make the experiment. In the third number some
verses of Davis's were published, but Dillon was discontented with his own production, and never could
be got to renew the attempt. It was in the sixth
number that Davis suddenly put forth his strength.
The night before publication he brought me the
"Lament of Owen Roe O'Neill," a ballad of singular originality and power. The dramatic opening
arrested attention like a sudden strain of martial
music :—

> " 'Did they dare, did they dare, to slay Owen Roe
>   O'Neill ? '
> 'Yes, they slew with poison him they feared to meet
>   with steel.'
> 'May God wither up their hearts ! may their blood cease
>   to flow !
> May they walk in living death who poisoned Owen
>   Roe.' "

The enthusiastic reception of this ballad by friends
whose judgment he trusted was like a revelation to
him. He came to understand that he possessed a
faculty till then unsuspected. He could express his
passionate convictions on the past, and his rapturous
reveries on the future, in the only shape in which they
would not appear extravagant or fantastic. He assumed the signature of "the Celt" to signify his
descent from the Welsh and Irish Gael, and it was

soon widely recognized that the soul of an old bardic
race throbbed again in his song. He recalled with
pride that the greatest modern lyrists—Béranger,
Moore, and perhaps Burns—were Celts, and, as he
insisted, brethren of the same family :

> " One in name and in fame
> Are the world-divided Gaels."*

But Burns was an utter Lowlander.

Strength comes to the strong and wealth to the
rich. After a little time, verses often as good as
Davis's or Mangan's flowed in from new contributors.
It was suggested in a provincial paper in the north
that the poetry of the *Nation* must be written by
Moore and the prose by Sheil and Carleton. And
the fourth number contained a paper which, when its
author made himself known (as he did in a little time),
rendered these wild stories probable. O'Connell,
who had not written anonymously in a newspaper for
nearly a generation, was so impressed by the astonishing success of the *Nation*, that he sent me a long and
vigorous paper entitled "A Repeal Catechism ;" and
John O'Connell returned to the fold, with a leading
article and a number of verses.†

* T. D. McGee.
† "Mr. Daunt brought in John O'Connell, who, as the
favourite son of the national leader, was counted an important
accession—for the prospectus at any rate ; but on the remon-

The success was vigorously pushed. The principal contributors met once a week at a frugal supper to exchange opinions and project the work of the coming week. These informal conferences proved a valuable training-school, less, perhaps, for what the young men taught each other than for what each taught himself. It is the silent process of rumination, doubtless, which determines the main lines of thought, but some men never know 'thoroughly their own opinions on a sub-ject till the train of slumbering reflection has been awakened by controversy, and the obscure points lighted by the sparks struck out in conflict. An illustrated gallery of distinguished Irishmen was com-menced, to set up anew on their pedestals our forgotten or neglected patriots ; feuilletons, original and trans-lated from the French, appeared in every number for a time ; and a system of " Answers to Correspondents," real and imaginary, was opened, in which new projects were broached, books and men briefly criticized, and seeds of fresh thought sown widely in the popular mind. The ballads and songs were our most unequivocal suc-cess, and Davis, who doubted at the outset the feasi-bility of the experiment, not only made the most

strance of some of the existing journalists, who considered them-selves injured by the publication of his name in that character, he separated from us before the issue of the first number, and only returned when to be a writer in the *Nation* had become a distinction worth coveting " (*Young Ireland*, chap. iii).

brilliant contributions to it, but interpreted its purpose most sympathetically.

"National poetry," he afterwards wrote, "presents the most dramatic events, the largest characters, the most impresive scenes, and the deepest passions in the language most familiar to us. It magnifies and ennobles our hearts, our intellects, our country, and our country-men ; binds us to the land by its condensed and gem-like history—to the future by example and by aspiration. It solaces us in travel, fires us in action, prompts our invention, sheds a grace beyond the power of luxury round our homes, is the recognized envoy of our minds among all mankind and to all time."

We had soon to repress a rage for versifying, often merely mimetic, sometimes as mechanical as the music of a barrel organ, which the success of the *Nation's* poets begot. Correspondents were told that the student who could rescue an Irish air or an Irish manuscript, or preserve an Irish ruin from destruction ; who could make a practical suggestion for bettering the social condition of the people, gather a fading tradition, throw light on an obscure era of our history, or help to instruct the people among whom he lived, would do a substantial and honourable service to his country, which need leave him no regret for wanting the gift of song. There was no mercy for nonsense, and the judgment on new verses or projects which the people applauded was often considered harsh and peremptory, the reader little suspecting that the merciless critic was often the author himself in masquerade.

The reception of the paper in the provinces was a perplexity to veteran journalists. From the first number it was received with an enthusiasm compounded. of passionate sympathy and personal affection. It went on increasing in circulation till its purchasers in every provincial town exceeded those of the local paper, and its readers were multiplied indefinitely by the practice of regarding it not as a vehicle of news but of opinion. It never grew obsolete, but passed from hand to hand till it was worn to fragments. The delight which young souls thirsting for nutriment found in it has been compared to the refreshment afforded by the sudden sight of a Munster valley in May after a long winter; but the unexpected is a large source of enjoyment, and it resembled rather the sight of a garden cooled by breezes and rivulets from the Nile, in the midst of a long stretch of sandbanks without a shrub or a blade of grass.

The doctrines which the new writers taught have a permanent interest, for they were the seed of many harvests to come. Though they were daring to rashness, and to timorous ears sounded like the tocsin of revolution, they were restrained by habitual submission to the eternal laws of morality and justice. Nothing was taught which was not, in their belief, intrinsically just and right, or which did not appeal to the noblest motives a generous but untaught people could be made to comprehend. Much of this teaching was the direct work of Davis ; but all his colleagues were busy completing the cosmos of Irish nationality, and a skilful critic will discern a variance of style, corresponding with variations of character of which natural style is a sure reflex.

The teaching might well constitute a primer of generous nationality.

"The restoration of Irish Independence," it was said, "has been advocated too exclusively by narrow appeals to economy, and sought by means which neither conciliated nor frightened its opponents. We shall try, and God willing we shall succeed in arraying the memories of our land, the deep, strong, passions of men's hearts, in favour of our cause. And while we shall shrink from repeating any factious or offensive cry, we shall counsel and explain those means of liberation which heroic freemen from Pelopidas to Washington have sanctioned.

"The restoration of land to the people had for a century no reason to support it save the musket of the ejected heir, desperate from suffering, and no witness save the peasant when the scaffold saw him martyred. We shall strive not merely to explain the workings of landlord misrule in Ireland, but to show how similar wrongs have been remedied in other countries ; seek to satisfy quiet intelligent men that the people cannot and ought not to be patient under the lash, and to urge such men to prevent the unguided vengeance of that people by leading them to redress.

"The people of Ireland are few enough for the size and capabilities of their country, but they are too many for its present state. They have no manufactures, there are no home-spent rents to give agricultural wages, there remains only the land; from that they are being ejected by the wicked and stupid scheme of consolidation, or, if left, it is under rack-rents, in wet wigwams, with rags not enough on their backs, and potatoes not enough for their food. If the Irish aristocracy persevere in exacting rack-rents, in clearing and consolidating; if absenteeism, want of employment and want of manufactures leave the people nothing between starvation in freedom or half-starvation in bondage in a workhouse,—if this come to pass, other things, not dreamed of just now, will follow.

"The popular organization is too exclusively political. It ought to be used for the creation and diffusion of national literature, vivid with the memories and hopes of a thoughtful and impassioned people. It may guide and encourage our countrymen, not only in all which concerns their libraries and lectures, but what is of greater importance, their music, their paintings, their public sports, those old schools of faith and valour.

"Men still speak of compromises, and material compensation for our lost nationality. But though Englishmen were to give us the best tenures on earth, though they were to equalize Presbyterian, Catholic, and Episcopalian, though they were to give us the completest representation in their Parliament, restore our absentees, disencumber us of their debt, and redress every one of our fiscal wrongs in the names of liberty and country, we would still tell them, in the name of enthusiastic hearts, thoughtful souls, and fearless spirits, that we spurned the gifts if the condition were that Ireland should remain a province."

Let it be remembered that O'Connell's doctrine
was that the Irish race were endowed with all good
gifts, physical and moral without stint, and were poor
and obscure only through the sins of their oppressors.
The *Nation* taught that to the evils inflicted on them
by misgovernment were added other evils created or
fostered by faults of their own. They wanted, not
only education and discipline, but the priceless habit
of perseverance. They had committed painful follies
and crimes, but they still possessed native virtue
which would infallibly redeem them at the cost of the
necessary labour and sacrifice.

"To make our liberty an inheritance for our children
and a charter of prosperity, the people must study as
well as strive, and learn as well as feel. Of all the
agencies of freedom, education was the most important.
It was in the mind of a people the seeds of future
greatness and prosperity were stored. The destruction
of her industry only made Ireland poor—the waste of
her mind left her a slave. Education, from being a
crime punishable with heavy penalties, became, under
the gradual change of weapons which tyranny was compelled to adopt, a wicked and deliberate scheme of
proselytism. There was still no system of national education adequate to the wants, and adapted to the genius
of our people. A little while ago there was none that
was not an insult and a curse.

"A people not familiar with the past would never
understand the present or realize the future. One of
the tasks the NATION humbly desired to perform was to

make the dead past familiar to the memory and imagination of the Irish people as the greatest and surest incentive to reclaim the control of their country; and not merely the past of their own country, but of the old and new worlds. The people did not recognize this imperative want. They were accustomed to consider themselves abreast or ahead of the rest of the world. The melancholy fact was that in all education—scholastic, social, and professional—they are behind most civilized nations. Energy, endurance, tenderness, piety, and faith—the natural elements of the highest moral and intellectual character—they still possessed as fresh as they existed in France or England centuries ago, in the ages of Faith and Action. But their best powers were unorganized and undeveloped, from want of that severe discipline so essential to bind in its harness the impetuous irregular vigour of our Celtic nature. A people with natural gifts which, under favourable circumstances, would produce not only artisans of the finest touch, but painters, musicians, and inventors, sweated under the heaviest toil in the world —felled the forests of Australia and drained the swamps of Canada.

"We Irish were INCURIOSO SUORUM. For ten who read MacGeoghegan a hundred read Leland, and for one who looked into the RERUM HIBERNICARUM SCRIPTORES a thousand studied Hume. Thus we judge our fathers by the calumnies of their foes. If Ireland were in national health, her history would be familiar by books, pictures, statuary, and music, to every cabin and workshop in the land; her resources, as an agricultural, manufacturing, and trading people, would be equally known; and every young man would be trained, and every grown man able to defend her coast, her plains, her towns, and her hills—not with his right arm merely,

but by his disciplined habits and military accomplishments.   These were the pillars of independence.

"Some of us were base enough to do cheerfully the
work of the enemy.   It was a mistake to imagine that
the only Irish hodmen in London were those poor fellows
who were always ascending and descending ladders with
bricks and mortar.   There were hodmen in Parliament,
who fetched and carried all sorts of rubbish for their
masters—newspaper hodmen, ready to knock their
country down with a brickbat—pamphleteering hodmen,
who get a despicable living by mixing dirty facts and
false figures together, and flinging them at Ireland,
wherever they see a chance of getting their mortar to
stick.   Thus we abandoned self-respect, and we were
treated with contempt; and nothing could be more
natural, nothing more just.   It is self-respect which
makes a people respected by others, as order makes them
strong, virtue formidable, patience victorious.

"Let Repealers, then, lift up their own souls, and
try by teaching and example to lift up the souls of
their family and neighbours to that pitch of industry,
courage, information, and wisdom necessary to enable an
enslaved, darkened, and starving people to become free,
enlightened, and prosperous.   And let them never forget what gifts and what zeal were needed to perform
that work effectually—what mildness to win, what
knowledge to inform, what reasoning to convince, what
vigour to rouse, what skill to combine and wield.   They
had been sometimes driven to employ the 'coward's
arms, trick, and chicane;' but they must renounce these
vices.   Extreme course might be necessary in the
struggle on which the country had entered, but dis-
honourable means never."

But the work of the journal was necessarily subor-

dinate to that of the national organization, and to this
it is now necessary to turn. O'Connell had rashly
promised that 1843 should be "the Repeal year"—
the year when his great object would be accomplished,
and he brought all the prodigious force of his will and
intellect to redeem this promise. Nature gave him
a physical vigour which labour could scarcely exhaust,
an imperturbable good temper, a courtesy before ad-
versaries, and a diplomacy which was dexterous and
versatile. Under these lay a subterranean rage against
injustice or opposition, which burst out at times like
a volcano. His passionate oratory in the Catholic
struggle raised the heart of the people as military
music refreshes and stimulates the weary soldier, and
this fire was not exhausted. Though he was tor
mented by the public and domestic troubles which a
man so placed rarely escapes—for cares gather round
the high-placed as clouds round the mountain summits
—he worked with unwavering perseverance. In Feb-
ruary he published a little volume in which the wrongs
inflicted on Ireland since the invasion were collected
from annals and records, and presented in one huge
indictment. In March he raised the national question by a motion before the Dublin Corporation, in a
speech of remarkable power and provident moderation. He was answered by Isaac Butt on behalf of
the Conservative party; and the controversy was con-

ducted with so much capacity and mutual forbearance, that it kindled desire and hope in many minds which long were apathetic.

Davis and the principal writers of the *Nation* were active members of the general committee of the Association. The ordinary business of a committee-man was to second, or, if he could not second, at least to echo the proposals of O'Connell. But the new men, as we have seen, had a policy and ideas of their own— a policy not designed to thwart, but to complete and consummate the purpose O'Connell aimed to accomplish. Davis hoped to enlist the middle class in the movement, and to inflame young men of both races with a national spirit. Dillon desired that the condition of the peasantry should receive immediate attention, and the question of land tenure and poor-laws to be promptly taken into consideration. Others had plans of systematic popular education and a legion of projects more or less practical for advancing the cause. They commenced to develop opinion, and to act on principles which have since become the common property of all enlightened Irishmen. There was naturally surprise and jealousy at the outset, but the new recruits were not men to whom it was possible to attribute sinister motives. Dillon was always sweet, placid, and open; and the transparent sincerity which looked out of Davis's large candid eyes, and from his

open, earnest face, dissipated suspicion; while an
energy that prompted him to engage in all the labour
of the largest designs and all the drudgery of the
minutest details disarmed jealousy. The result was
a transformation scene which only those who have
witnessed it with their eyes will fully understand. In
the midst of the old traditional agitation, grown de-
crepid and somewhat debauched, a new power claimed
recognition. The servile and illiterate agitators who
acknowledged no law but the will of their leader, saw
among them men of original ideas and commanding
intellect, who pressed their opinions on their audience
with becoming modesty indeed, but without the
smallest fear or hesitation.

Davis avoided wounding dangerous susceptibilities
less from policy than from the generosity and modesty
of his nature; and, at this time, O'Connell certainly
felt that he had got colleagues whose ability and zeal
would do effective service, though they did not always
run in the traditional harness. Looking back through
the rarified atmosphere of experience, I cannot insist
that all our designs were discreet or practical. We
were defeated by a narrow majority on the proposal to
maintain an agent in Paris, as the centre of political
activity in Europe, which, had it been accepted, would
certainly have been savagely misrepresented by the
enemies of the national cause. O'Connell's sons were

at times defeated in the Committee on questions arising between them and the new men, and once or twice O'Connell himself had to accept proposals which he did not entirely relish. The practical man of the world bore a slight reverse with a good humour which disarmed opposition ; for he knew the proposals were always designed to feed the flame of nationality.

Much was done to enlarge and vitalize the old traditional system. An historical and political library of reference was collected, peculiarly rich in the rare Anti-Union and Emancipation pamphlets. The cards of membership were made an agency for teaching the people national history and statistics, and familiarizing them with the effigies of their great men. A band was trained to play national airs in public for the first time since the Union. And Repeal wardens were exhorted to watch over historic ruins in their district, and to encourage the people to found news-rooms and local societies.

We are apt to regard as trite and commonplace the transactions of our own day, but drape these young men like Rienzi in the forum or like the Swiss foresters who led the Alpine spears at Morgartan, and they become picturesque and heroic. Rightly understood, the work they had undertaken was of the same scope and magnitude, though it was not projected in the gloom of forests or the shade of august ruins, but under the glare of sunshine in committee rooms and news-paper offices, by men clothed in paletots and chimney-pot hats.

After the serious business of life began, Davis had no longer leisure for elaborate correspondence. He wrote constantly to a chosen few, but only notes as brief as bulletins. His mind produced abundantly the fresh fancies, the just reflections, and the graceful badinage which make the charm of perfect letters, but all went to swell the stream of public work, on which his heart was set. His correspondence is valuable chiefly because it tells us what he was doing, and thinking of, and makes plain the unbroken purpose of his life.

To Maddyn he wrote most habitually. He desired to engage him in a project for a high-class periodical on Federalistic principles—Federalism being then much spoken of among National Whigs as a possible compromise.

"Enclosed are some suggestions for NATION papers, by Duffy, which of course you'll accept, change, or reject, as you like. Munster Society would give you fine subjects—sketches of classes of characters. Now to your letter.

"The party who would sustain the REVIEW are Federalists—men thoroughly national in feeling, catholic in taste, and moderate in politics. Things have come to that pass that we must be disgraced and defeated, or we must separate by force, or we must have a

Federal Government. Mere repeal is raw and popular.
The Federalists include all who were Whigs in Belfast,
the best of your Cork men, Wyse, Caulfield, and
several excellent men through the country. Hudson
and Torrens McCullagh, Deasy, Wallis, and all that
set are Federalists. I will not ask you to come until
matters are fixed and safe and clear; all I wished now
was to know might you come? You would make a great,
a perfect editor. We must parochialize the people by
property and institutions, and idealize and soften them
by music, history, ballad, art, and games. That is, if
we succeed, and are not hanged instead; but I KNOW
my principles will succeed."

After the Corporation debate the Repeal Association
received important recruits and a great accession of
friends, and it was determined to summon a muster
of the whole population in each of the counties in succession. These assemblies were so gigantic that the
Times described them as "monster meetings"—a
title which they retained. During the summer the
monster meetings increased in number and enthusiasm,
and the Irish Tories called upon the Government to
check them by some sharp stroke of authority. Sir
Edward Sugden, an English lawyer, at that time Lord
Chancellor of Ireland, answered their appeal by removing Lord Ffrench and four and twenty other
magistrates from the Commission of the Peace, for the
new offence of attending public meetings in favour of
the Repeal of the Union. Mr. Smith O'Brien, till
then known as an Irish Whig of popular sympathies,

inquired in Parliament if the same discipline was to be extended to English magistrates ; and not getting a satisfactory reply, he resigned his commission, which could no longer, he conceived, be held by an Irish gentleman without humiliation. Lord Cloncurry, Henry Grattan, and a number of other country gentle·men followed his example. The Bar struck a more effectual stroke. Twenty barristers joined the Association in one day as a protest against the unconstitutional character of an executive who degraded magistrates for taking one side of a debatable public question, while they applauded other magistrates for taking the opposite side. Among these recruits were Thomas O'Hagan, afterwards Lord Chancellor ; Sir Colman O'Loghlen, afterwards Judge Advocate-General ; and Thomas MacNevin, and M. J. Barry— the two latter of whom from that time became constant associates of the young men of the *Nation*.

In answer to some remonstrance on the rashness of his policy, Davis wrote to Maddyn :—

"You seem to me to underrate our resources. The Catholic population are more united, bold, and orderly than ever they were. Here are materials for defence or attack, civil or military. The hearty junction of the Catholic bishops is of the greatest value. The Protestants of the lower order are neutral ; the land question and repeated disappointments from England have alienated them from their old views. Most of the educated Protestants now profess an ardent nationality, and say that, if some pledge against a Catholic ascendancy could be given them, they too would be Repealers. You will see by the accompanying paper that fourteen barristers, most of them men of good business, joined yesterday. The Americans are constantly offering us men, money, and arms. . . . Crowds of soldiers and police are enrolled Repealers. These are some of our resources. The present agitation will not fail for want of statesmanship, though it may for want of energy. Even O'Connell has looked very far ahead this time, and he knows he cannot retreat. I think we can beat Peal. If we can quietly get a Federal Government I shall for one agree to it and support it. If not, then anything but what we are."

Davis's character is exhibited, not only in what he did and wrote, but in the echoes of it which came back to him from friends, even when they took the character of objections or remonstrances. Denny Lane wrote at this time :—

"Short, narrative, and NOT descriptive, ballads are greatly wanted in Irish literature. By all means stick to poetry, but pray do not abandon professional success —you are fully equal to two strong pursuits. If you should meet political disappointment, your literary talents and poetical longings will always keep existence fresh."

Maddyn applauded an attempt which I had recently made to expose the ignorance and dishonesty of the school of pseudo-Irish romances then becoming popular in England.

"I have read with delight an article in the NATION on Lever's works. It is most admirably done; whoever the writer is, he has certainly displayed no ordinary literary abilities; and never did any Irish writer deserve more richly the treatment he has met with at the hands of honest Irish criticism. I cannot conceive the spurious liberality which affects to patronize the anti-national tendencies of all this man's writings, on account of the rollicking devil-may-care sort of factious fun and ferocious drollery of his slipshod, flimsy, fashionable, novelish style of writing."*

The *Nation*, while it urged on the monster meetings and the entire O'Connell programme, never neglected its individual policy. It was a puzzle to the people to find Irishmen of genius honoured and applauded without any regard to their political opinions. Up to that time the popular test was simply the relation of a man to the great tribune. If he hurrahed for O'Connell with sufficient vehemence, much was forgiven him in conduct and opinion; if he criticized the darling of the nation, scarcely any service was an adequate set off. Even Moore fell into disfavour for singing, in one of his later melodies, the decay of public spirit in Ireland.

This uniform courtesy and firmness towards opponents, though it was new in Irish controversy, did not offend popular feeling, because it was accom-

* June 10, 1843. The article was entitled " Plunderings and Blunderings of Harry Lorrequer."

panied by an unsparing exposure of the system they maintained. Though it was a main aim of the young men to reconcile the gentry and the Protestant minority with the whole nation, it was an aim never pursued by ignoring the intolerable injustice of the Established Church and the existing land system. " Be just, and you shall be the acknowledged leaders of a devoted people ; but justice must be done, for they are withering under your exactions." This was the language held. The gentry were told that they had never done their duty, and that their neglect of it lay at the root of Irish misery. The land system which they had framed in the Irish Parliament seemed an instrument of torture needlessly stringent for a people so broken and dependent, but, like a great bridge over a small stream, it gave the measure of the slumbering force which it was intended to restrain. The awakening of this force was the object of their constant apprehension, and it was now appealed to weekly with ideas that struck it like electric shocks. The *Nation* taught as axioms that the land was not the landlord's own to do as he would with, but could only be held in proprietorship subject to the prior claim of the inhabitants to get food and clothing out of it. No length of time and no solemnity of sanction could annul the claim of the husbandman to eat the fruit of his toil, or transfer the claim to a select circle of landed proprietors. Why should landlords be the only class of traders above the law? There was no more inherent sanctity in selling land, or hiring it out, than in selling shoes; and the trader in acres ought to be as amenable to the law, and as easily punished for extortion as his humbler brother. The existing system had lasted long indeed, but fraud and folly were not consecrated by time, they only grew grosser fraud and more intolerable folly. The landlord was entitled to a fair rent for the usufruct of his land; all claims beyond this, over the tenant's time, conscience, or opinions, were extortion or usurpation.

It would be unskilful criticism to judge the verses Davis wrote in intervals of this busy and stormy life by the canons we apply to a poet in his solitude. His aims were far away from literary success All his labours tended only to stimulate and discipline the people, and his dearest hope was to take part in guiding the counsels of a nation which he had prompted into action and marshalled to victory. The place he would have loved to fill was not beside Moore and Goldsmith, but beside O'Neill and Grattan.

A song or ballad was struck off at a heat, when a flash of inspiration came,—scrawled with a pencil, in a large hand, on a sheet of post-paper, with unfinished lines, perhaps, and blanks for epithets which did not come at once of the right measure or colour; but the chain of sentiment or incident was generally complete. If there was time it was revised later and copied once more with pen and ink, and last touches added before it was despatched to the printer ; but if occasion demanded, it went at once.   For his verses were written to make Irishmen understand and love Ireland, as the poet understood and loved her.   What Robert Burns wrote of his own purpose and inspiration as a poet, Davis might have written of himself, changing only the nationality.

"Scottish scenes and Scottish story are the themes I wish to sing. I have no dearer aim than to make leisurely pilgrimages through Caledonia, to sit on the fields of her battles, to wander on the romantic banks of her rivers, and to muse by the stately towers or venerable ruins once the honoured abodes of her heroes."*

And in one sense he was more of a national poet than any of the illustrious writers whom I have named : he embraced the whole nation in his sympathy. Béranger scorned and detested a party which formed a substantial minority of his countrymen ; Moore scarcely recognised the existence of a peasantry in his national melodies ; even Burns, a Lowland poet, had imperfect sympathy with the natives of the mountains among whom Walter Scott was to find his heroes. But Davis loved and sang the whole Irish people.

* Robert Burns's letter to Mrs. Dunlop.

"Here came the proud Phœnician, the man of trade
and toil—
Here came the proud Milesian, a-hungering for spoil;
And the Firbolg and the Cymry, and the hard, enduring Dane,
And the iron Lords of Normandy, with the Saxons in
their train.

"And oh! it were a gallant deed to show before mankind,
How every race and every creed might be by love
combined—
Might be combined, yet not forget the fountains whence
they rose,
As, filled by many a rivulet, the stately Shannon flows."

But the native rulers who held their own for centuries against the invader touched him closest. Here
are a few verses from a vigorous and picturesque
ballad entitled, "A True Irish King"—

"The Cæsar of Rome has a wider domain,
And the ARD RIGH of France has more clans in his
train,
The sceptre of Spain is more heavy with gems,
And our crowns cannot vie with the Greek diadems;
But kinglier far, before heaven and man,
Are the Emerald fields, and the fiery-eyed clan,
The sceptre, and state, and the poets who sing,
And the swords that encircle A TRUE IRISH KING."

"For he must have come from a conquering race—
The heir of their valour, their glory, their grace:
His frame must be stately, his step must be fleet,
His hand must be trained to each warrior feat,

H

His face, as the harvest moon, steadfast and clear,
A head to enlighten, a spirit to cheer;
While the foremost to rush where the battle-brands
    ring,
And the last to retreat is A TRUE IRISH KING !"

It is curious how soon and how thoroughly this town-bred bookish man caught the characteristics of social life in an Irish village. Griffin or Carleton could scarcely surround a modest Irish girl about to become a bride with more characteristic incidents than these:—

"We meet in the market and fair—
    We meet in the morning and night—
He sits on the half of my chair,
    And my people are wild with delight.
Yet I long through the winter to skim,
    Though Eoghan longs more, I can see,
When I will be married to him,
    And he will be married to me.
        Then, oh! the marriage, the marriage,
           With love and *mo buachaill* for me!
        The ladies that ride in a carriage,
           Might envy the marriage of me."

There is not, I think, in the lyrics of Burns a more spontaneous gush of natural feeling in unstudied words than this song of a peasant girl :—

"His kiss is sweet, his word is kind,
    His love is rich to me;
I could not in a palace find
    A truer heart than he.

The eagle shelters not his nest
  From hurricane and hail
More bravely than he guards my breast—
  This Boatman of Kinsale.

"The brawling squires may heed him not,
  The dainty stranger sneer—
But who will dare to hurt our cot,
  When Myles O'Hea is here?
The scarlet soldiers pass along;
  They'd like, but fear to rail;
His blood is hot, his blow is strong—
  The Boatman of Kinsale."

In these ballads he is never guilty of the bad taste of undervaluing the enemy with whom his people struggle. How fine is this picture of the English column at Fontenoy!—

"Six thousand English veterans in stately column tread,
Their cannon blaze in front and flank, Lord Hay is at
    their head
Steady they step a-down the slope—steady they climb
    the hill;
Steady they load—steady they fire, moving right onward
    still,
Betwixt the wood and Fontenoy, as through a furnace
    blast,
Through rampart, trench, and palisade, and bullets
    showering fast;
And on the open plain above they rose, and kept their
    course,
With ready fire and grim resolve, that mocked at
    hostile force:

Past Fontenoy, past Fontenoy, while thinner grow their
    ranks—
They break, as broke the Zuyder Zee through Holland's
    ocean banks.

"More idly than the summer flies, French tirailleurs
    rush round;
As stuble to the lava tide, French squadrons strew the
    ground;
Bomb-shell, and grape, and round-shot tore, still on they
    marched and fired—
Fast, from each volley, grenadier and voltigeur retired.
'Push on, my household cavalry!' King Louis madly
    cried:
To death they rush, but rude their shock—not un-
    avenged they died.
On through the camp the column trod—King Louis
    turns his rein:
'Not yet, my liege,' Saxe interposed, 'the Irish troops
    remain;'
And Fontenoy, famed Fontenoy, had been a Waterloo,
Were not these exiles ready then, fresh, vehement, and
    true."

The number of poems produced in three years
supply evidence of his singular fertility. Moore, we
know from his diary, spent day after day over one of his
"Irish Melodies." Béranger with the same frankness
describes the prolonged labour a song cost him; half
a dozen a year were as many as he could finish to his
satisfaction. Davis in the midst of engrossing political
labours, produced three times as many—nearly fifty in
three years; and his friends might place the "Battle

of Fontenoy," or the "Sack of Baltimore," beside "Remember the glories of Brian the Brave," or "Le Chant du Cosaque," as confidently as Turner hung one of his landscapes side by side with a Claude.

The young men who had yet no political designation or nickname to distinguish them were drawn more and more together by personal sympathy. The connection grew as political connections are apt to grow; they had a common stock of opinions, a journal to express them, much social intercourse, leaders whom they trusted, and opposition enough to discipline and consolidate their union.

A weekly supper was held at each other's houses in succession, to preserve the sentiment of equality and fraternity. It was a council table in effect, where every one brought his intellectual offering of frank criticism, practical suggestion, story or song, and might be sure of unstinted recognition; for this friendly gathering of men running the same race was as free from envy or rivalry as any assembly of men ever was on the earth. Every one was busy in a common cause, and a brotherhood of design is the poetry of what in ordinary circumstances is mere *esprit de corps.* Davis was a peer among his peers, never aiming at any lead that was not spontaneously accorded him, and scarcely accepting that much without demur. He loved to be loved, but he was totally indifferent to popularity, and is dis-

tinguished from all Irish tribunes who preceded him
or have followed him by a perfectly genuine desire to
remain unknown, and reap neither recognition nor reward from his work.   Thinkers who habitually debate
the serious interests of life are apt to oppress their
audience by the gravity of their speech.   But Davis's
conversation was cheerful and natural, and his demean-
our familiar and winning.

At this time he was under thirty years of age, a
strongly built, middle-sized man, with beaming face, a
healthy glow, and deep blue eyes, set in a brow of solid
strength.   His countenance was agreeable from expression rather than from contour, and was habitually
lighted up with sincerity and cordiality.   There was a
manly carelessness in his bearing, as of one who, though
well-dressed, never thought of dress or appearance.
When he accidentally met a friend, he had the habit of
throwing back his head to express a pleased surprise,*
which was very winning ; a voice not so much sonorous
as sympathetic, a cordial laugh and cheerful eyes completed the charm.

The most surprising characteristic of his talk was its
simplicity.   He was never a colloquial athlete, making

---

* "I see that start of glad surprise,
   The lip comprest, the moistened eyes ;
   I hear his deep impressive tone,
   And feel his clasp, a brother's own " (O'Hagan).

happy hits and adroit fences; he spoke chiefly of the interests of the hour with plainness and sincerity, but his opinions were apt to come out in sentences which would be remembered for their significance or solidity. When moved, which was rarely, he spoke with a proud, earnest sententiousness, which was very impressive. There were men among his associates, and men of notable ability, who announced a new opinion like a challenge to controversy, but Davis ordinarily dropped it out like a platitude, on which it was needless to pause. He loved to condense a cardinal truth into a familiar winning phrase, as much as some men love to fabricate a novelty out of a maxim of Epictetus, or an epigram of Rochefoucauld. To circulate truth was his object, never to appropriate it and stamp his own name on it. He naturally spoke much, as he wrote much, for he had a fulness of life which broke out at all the intellectual pores; and his talk had a flavour of wide reading and careful thought, like the olives and subtle salt which give its piquancy to a French *plat*. He never spoke as a leader or pedagogue, but always as a comrade, and as a natural result he was loved as much as he was trusted. To be original, to be deeply in earnest, and at the same time to be loved, supposes rare qualities, not only in the man but in his consociates, for few men can endure to be taught. They sought his counsel in difficulties, and always found more than they sought. In political conferences it was impossible not to remark a certain abrupt, but not discourteous dogmatism, but in a *tête-à-tête* not a trace of it remained :—

> "He spoke and words more soft than rain,
> Brought back the age of gold again."*

If ever there was a gleam of anger in his eyes you might be sure it was wrath against some intolerable wrong, like the pious rage of Dante. It was never passionate ; his temper was perfect. I have seen him tried by unreasonable pretensions, by petulant complaints, by contemptuous dissent from what he held most certain and sacred, but he maintained a sweet composure and was master of himself. In these trials nature had need to be repressed by a disciplined will, for beads of perspiration on his broad brow often disclosed the contest within ; but angry word or gesture none of his comrades ever saw. Starting from the perfectly just assumption that they loved and trusted him, he made light of dissent. Controversy he knew was one of the processes by which opinion is created or regulated, and a man often modifies his opinions in the very act of defending them. Even his enthusiasm, which was singularly contagious, was regulated and restrained'

* Emerson.

never clamorous or aggressive. Celtic Irishmen have a tendency to take offence easily and to stand upon their dignity quite gratuitously ; his example tended to correct this weakness, and if it exhibited itself he encountered it with a grave sweet courtesy which made the offender ashamed of himself.

Like Fox he was a " very painstaking man," and this quality never exhibited itself so assiduously as in the service of his companions. When he promised anything, however trivial, or made a casual rendezvous, one could count on a definite fulfilment—not a common characteristic of gifted young Celts. He loved to make his knowledge their common property. When he met in his readings a new book which enlarged his horizon of political knowledge, or suggested some new device for serving the cause, he exhibited such generous rapture that he roused congenial feelings among his associates, and inspired even the sceptical with some of his ardour of study and hopeful views of life.

I must speak of our weekly supper. MacCarthy was our Sydney Smith. His humour was as spontaneous as sunshine, and often flashed out as unexpectedly in grave debate as a sunbeam from behind a mask of clouds. Some practical man proposed that there should be a close season for jokes, but they did not impede business, but rather seasoned it and made it palatable. MacNevin and Barry were wits, and sayers of good things; MacCarthy was a genuine humourist. MacNevin's mirth was explosive, and sometimes went off without notice, like steam from a safety-valve. Barry uttered his good things with a gravity which set off their dry humour, and was accused of preparing the *mise en scène*. Denny Lane, on some such occasion, told a story of one of his fellow-citizens who used to produce a pun once a year, and gave a dinner party to let it off, sometimes getting up appropriate scenery, machinery, and decorations for the new birth, which turned his annual into a little melodrama.

Davis was never a *faiseur de phrases*, but sayings of force or significance sometimes fell from him spontaneously. Some one quoted Plunket's saying that to certain men history was no better than an old almanac. "Yes," he replied, "and under certain other conditions an old almanac becomes an historical romance." I brought to breakfast with him one morning a young Irish-American recruit, burning to know personally the men who had drawn him across the Atlantic, and possessing himself many of the gifts he loved in them. I asked Davis next day how he liked Darcy McGee. "With time I might like him," he said, "but he seemed too much bent on *transacting* an acquaintance with me." A certain new recruit brought a pocketful of projects, good, bad, and indifferent, some of them indeed excellent, but he exhibited them as if they were the Sibyl's books. Speaking of him next day, some one said that his talk was like champagne. "No," said Davis, "not like champagne, like seidlitz-powder; it is effervescent and wholesome, but one never gets rid of the idea that it is physic." But though he had a keen enjoyment of pleasantry, and loved banter and badinage, he did not possess the faculty of humour. When he occasionally made experiments in this region he became satirical or savage. Like Schiller, he looked habitually at the graver aspect of human affairs, and was too much in earnest for the disengaged mind and easy play of faculties necessary to be sportive. But if we judged Burns by his epigrams, how low he would be rated.

The youngest of the associates were John O'Hagan[*] and John Pigot. O'Hagan was a law student, labouring to acquire the mastery of principles which alone makes the law a liberal and philosophical profession. He was modest and reticent, speaking rarely, and never of himself or his works. MacCarthy, in his poem of the "Lay Missionary," has painted his social life. In literature he made himself

---

[*] The late Mr. Justice O'Hagan, head of the Land Commission in Ireland.

gradually known to his colleagues by sound criticism in the sweetest of wholesome English, and by poems which constantly extended the range of his powers into new regions. John Pigot was a bright handsome boy, son of an eminent Whig lawyer afterwards Chief Baron of the Exchequer, and Davis held him in great affection. He was a diligent and zealous student, and a perpetual missionary of national opinions in good society. He contributed sometimes, but very rarely, to the *Nation*, for he was not as yet a writer of the requisite vigour or skill for that office.

O'Callaghan was older than his colleagues, and of another school. He had gone through the first Repeal agitation, and had never quite recovered from its disillusions. He was a tall, dark, strong man, who spoke a dialect compounded apparently in equal parts from Johnson and Cobbett, in a voice too loud for social intercourse. "I love," he would cry, "not the entremets of literature, but the strong meat and drink of sedition," or, "I make a daily meal on the smoked carcase of Irish history." Some one affirmed that he heard him instructing his partner in a dance on the exact limits of the Irish pentarchy and the malign slander of Giraldus Cambrensis. O'Callaghan was a thoroughly honest man, but he brought into Irish politics in his train a younger brother, whose sly furtive character none of the young men could tolerate. He was never admitted to the weekly suppers, never permitted to write a line in the *Nation*. He betook himself to other associates and other journals, and, in the end, ripened into a Government spy.

Mangan never came to the weekly suppers, and I had to invent opportunities of making him known to a few of our colleagues one by one. He had the shyness of a man who lives habitually apart, and the soreness of one whose sensitive nerves have suffered in contact with the rude world. Like Balzac, Scribe, and Disraeli, he commenced life in an attorney's office, and was tortured by the practical jokes and exuberant spirits of his companions.

William Carleton,* whom I had known for many years, called at the *Nation* office from time to time to criticize or applaud what we were doing, and in the end to help us. He was cordially received by the young men, invited to excursions which we made to historical places, fêted and encouraged to become frankly a Nationalist; but it is a significant fact that to the weekly suppers, which were our cabinet council, he never found his way. He liked the men cordially, found their talk agreeable and their histori-

* Author of *Traits and Stories of the Irish Peasants*, etc.

cal excursions, pleasant picnics, at any rate, but their purpose was something which, with all his splendid equipment of brains, he was incapable of comprehending.

Davis was my senior in age, and greatly more my senior in knowledge and experience. Educated in a city, disciplined in a university, living habitually in society where he had friends and competitors of his own age and condition, he got the training which develops the natural forces in the healthiest manner. I had lived in a small country town, where I had not the good fortune to encounter one associate of similar tastes and studies, except Henry MacManus, the artist, and T. B. MacManus, who has left an honourable name in Irish annals ; and I had paid the penalty of being a Catholic in Ireland by being withheld from a university which still maintains the agencies of proselytism and the insolence of ascendancy. I took my new friend into my heart of hearts, where he maintained the first place from that day forth.

The young men had as yet no visible following, and might be described in the contemptuous language which Jefferson flung at the friends of Alexander Hamilton, " as a party all head and no body." But the future Young Irelanders were estimated as unskilfully as the future Federalists; for, like them, they grew into a decisive power. Even at that time there was a surrounding of youngsters who neither wrote nor harangued, but constituted a sympathetic chorus, almost as essential to the success of the drama as the actors themselves. They sang their songs, repeated their *mots*, carried their opinions into society, and sometimes quite honestly mistook them for their own.

Whenever men are combined for a large purpose, good or evil, posterity is apt to select one of them to inherit all the honour. In the Reformation we think only of Luther, but without Calvin and Knox the Reformation might have remained a German schism. Of the Jesuits the world remembers chiefly St. Ignatius, but he was far from being the first in genius, or even in governing power, of that marvellous company. Among the forerunners of the French Revolution opinion settles upon Rousseau and Voltaire, but Denis Diderot sapped the buttresses of authority and stubbed the roots of faith with a more steadfast and malign industry. Wilberforce is hailed emancipator of the negroes, but without Clarkson and Zachary Macaulay he would have gone to his grave without seeing their fetters struck off. Original men come in groups, and so it was now. Davis was the truest type of his generation, not because he was most gifted, but because his whole faculties were devoted to his work; and because he was not one-sided, but a complete and consummate man. But the era produced a crowd of notable persons. Mangan was a truer poet, but he altogether wanted the stringent will which made Davis's work so fruitful. Ferguson's literary range was wider, and his work was more artistically handled, but he shrunk from allying himself in aims and interests with the bulk of the people. MacNevin, and still more in later times Meagher, uttered appeals more eloquent and touching, but each of them kindled his torch at the living fire of Davis. Dillon had, perhaps, a safer judgment, and certainly a surer appreciation of difficulties; but his labours were intermittent. Most of their separate qualities united in some considerable degree in Davis, and every faculty was applied with unwavering purpose to a single end, which ruled his life "like a guiding star above."

Irish history had been shamefully neglected in school and college, and the young men took up the teaching of it in the *Nation;* not as a cold scientific analysis, but as a passionate search for light which might help them to understand their own race and country. When this attempt began, Irish history was rather less known than Chinese. A mandarin implied a definite idea; but what was a Tanist? Confucius was a wise man among the Celestials; but who was Moran? One man out of ten thousand could not tell whether Owen

Roe followed or preceded Brien Boroihime; in which hemisphere the victory of Benburb was achieved; or whether the O'Neill who held Ireland for eight years in the Puritan wars was a naked savage armed with a stake, or an accomplished soldier bred in the most adventurous and punctilious service in Europe. They speedily lighted up this obscure past with a sympathy which gilded it like sunshine, till the study of our annals became a passion with young Irishmen. On this teaching Davis constantly strove to impress a precise aim and purpose. He ransacked the past, not to find weapons of assault against England, still less to feed the lazy reveries of seannachies and poets upon legends of a golden age hid in the mists of antiquity, but to rear a generation whose lives would be strengthened and ennobled by the knowledge that there had been great men of their race, and great actions done on the soil they trod; whose resolution and fidelity would be fortified by knowing that their ancestors had left their mark for ever on some of the most memorable eras of European history; that they were heirs to a litany of soldiers, scholars, and ecclesiastics, no more fabulous or questionable than the marshals of Napoleon or the poets of Weimar; and to warn them by the light of the past of the perilous vices and weaknesses which had so often betrayed our people.

We were warned by the *Times*, and a chorus of

I

smaller critics, that these historical reminiscences fostered national animosities. Perhaps they did; but is there any method of exposing great wrongs which does not beget indignation against the wronger? We were of opinion that writers who habitually employed the epithet Swiss to signify a mercenary, Greek a cheat, Jew a miser, Turk a brute, and Yankee a pedlar, who used the phrase "Dutch courage" to signify drunkenness, and a "Flemish account" to signify deception, who symbolized a Frenchman as a fop, and a French woman as a hag (beldam=belle dame), and who called whatsoever was stupid or foolish Irish—an Irish argument being an argument that proved nothing, and an Irish method a method which was bound to fail— were scarcely entitled to take us to task for truths which, however disagreeable, were at least authentic.

The journal alone was not a sufficient agent for this purpose, and books to fill some of the greater voids in our history began to appear. The work which the young men did in this way was of wider scope and greater permanence than anything they could accomplish in the Association. They were slowly, half unconsciously, laying the foundations of a national literature. Their first experiment was a little sixpenny brochure, printed at the *Nation* office, and sold by the *Nation* agents—a collection of the songs and ballads published during three months, entitled *The Spirit of the Nation.* Its success was a marvel. The Conservatives set the example of applauding its ability, while they condemned its aim and spirit. Frederick Shaw, then leader of the Irish Tories, read specimens to the House of Commons as a warning of a new danger. Isaac Butt, his rival in Ireland, made the little book the main subject of his speech at a Conservative meeting in Dublin, and declared the writer —assuming the book to be the production of one man instead of a dozen—"deserved the name and had the inspiration of a poet." And Mr. LeFanu, the most gifted journalist of the party, taking the prose and poetry together, pronounced the *Nation* to be the most ominous and formidable phenomenon of strange and terrible times.

"The NATION," he added, "is written with a masculine vigour, and with an impetuous singleness of purpose which makes every number tell home. It represents the opinions and feelings of some millions of men, reflected with vivid precision in its successive pages, and, taken for all in all, it is a genuine and gigantic representative of its vast party."

This interest, curiously compounded of anger and sympathy, spread to England. John Wilson Croker, in the *Quarterly Review*, praised without stint "the beauty of language and imagery," but declared, in his habitual slashing style, that "they exhibited the deadliest rancour, the most audacious falsehoods, and the most incendiary provocations to war." The *Times* affirmed that O'Connell's mischievous exhortations were tame compared with the fervour of rebellion which breathed in every page of these verses. The echo of those strong opinions ran through the chief critical and political journals, and the *Naval and Military Gazette* added a dash of vitriol to the flame when it announced that the songs made their way into the barracks, and were sung at the public houses frequented by Irish soldiers. The newspaper office could not produce the book fast enough for the demand, and at an early period I transferred it to Mr. James Duffy, a publisher then in a small way of business in a by-street, to whom it was the beginning of great prosperity. Remembering the precedent of Robert Burns, who refused to make money by the songs of his country, we made a free gift of the little book to the publisher.

The second experiment was a collection of the orators of Ireland. It was designed to bring into one series the greatest speeches of the men who fought the battle of parliamentary independence in the eighteenth century; next, the great Irishmen who had served the Empire with conspicuous ability—Burke, Canning, and Wellesley; and, finally, of the two tribunes of the Catholic agitation, O'Connell and Shiel.

Davis began the series with a collection of Curran's

speeches, prefaced by a fresh, vigorous, and sparkling memoir. The book has since run through twenty editions, and is in the hands of every student of Irish history. It had to encounter the conceited dogmatism which a work of original genius seldom escapes, but we can read this rash disparagement with something of the sensation which Brougham's estimate of Byron, or Jeffrey's of Wordsworth, or John Wilson's of Tennyson is apt to create in a reader of to-day. It used to be said with some justice that if you put an Irishman to roast, another Irishman would turn the spit. The turnspit on this occasion was Mr. Marmion Savage, a gentleman who commenced his career at the Corn Exchange declaiming against tithe, and ended as clerk of the Privy Council. He pronounced judgment on Davis's volume in the *Athenæum*, and the opening paragraph is worth preserving as one of the curiosities of criticism.

"A greener book than this has not yet issued from the Green Isle. The cover is greener than the shamrock; the contents greener again; and the style and execution are green in the superlative degree. In short, it is 'one entire and perfect EMERALD,' saving the value of that precious stone. It must needs be an emanation from some very green and unripe genius, who sees every object through a pair of green spectacles; nay, we have a suspicion that the author is no other than the actual Green Man."

MacNevin followed Davis with a collection of the State Trials in Ireland from 1794 to 1803—the era of Castlereagh and Carhampton—lighted up with a vivid introduction. A popular edition of MacGeoghegan's *History of Ireland* followed—a valuable book, published in Paris by an emigrant priest,—and Barrington's *Rise and Fall of the Irish Nation*, and Foreman's famous *Defence of the Courage, Honour, and Loyalty of the Irish*—the last edited by Davis.

Every week the journal contained counsel to young Irishmen on education, discipline, the use they might make of their lives, and the services they could perform for their country, and the same spirit animated their work in the Association.

"Watch over our historical places," they said; "they are in the care of the people, and they are ill-cared. All classes, creeds, and politics are to blame in this. The peasant lugs down a pillar for his sty, the farmer for his gate, the priest for his chapel, the minister for his glebe. A mill-stream ran through Lord Moore's Castle, and the commissioners of Galway have shaken, and threatened to remove, the Warden's house, that fine stone chronicle of Galway heroism. [A warden of Galway was the Brutus of Ireland, and sacrificed his son to his country.] But these ruins were rich possessions. The state of civilization among our Scotic, or Milesian, or Norman, or Danish sires, was better seen from a few raths, keeps, and old coast towns, with the help of the Museum of the Irish Academy, than from all the prints and historical novels we have. An old castle in Kilkenny, a house in Galway give us a peep at the arts, the intercourse, the creed, the indoor, and some of the out-door ways of the gentry of the one, and of the merchants of the other, clearer than Scott could, were he to write, or Cattermole, were he to paint for forty years. Yet year after year more of our crosses are broken, of our tombs effaced, of our abbeys shattered, of our castles torn down, of our cairns sacrilegiously pierced, of our urns broken up, and of our coins melted down."

All this work had to be done with a constant watchfulness against giving offence to the national leader, who had small sympathy with the philosophy or poetry of politics, and a general disrelish of unauthorized experiments.

The monster meetings went on with unflagging spirit and still increasing numbers. Many millions of Irishmen had now been paraded and battalioned as Nationalists determined at all costs to raise up their country anew. The influence of a resolute organized people was tremendous. It made itself felt in every fibre of the nation, among the most hostile section as well as the most sympathetic. Here are two or three significant illustrations. The Repeal members were required to attend the meetings of the Association, and in their absence the Government proposed an Arms Bill of unexampled stringency; but the public spirit was alert, and it was resisted by Irish Whigs, led on this occasion by Lord Clements, Sharman Crawford,

and Smith O'Brien with stubborn persistence. Half
of the session was wasted before it was forced through
the Commons.

When these Irish Liberals had failed in Parliament
they addressed themselves directly to the English
people, inviting them to consider the condition to
which the fatal policy which England supported had
reduced Ireland. The people were poor, estranged,
and exasperated by a long course of vicious legisla-
tion. The labouring population lived habitually on
the verge of destitution. Irish commerce, manufactures, fisheries, mines, and agriculture attested by
their languishing and neglected condition the baneful
effects of misgovernment. Was there any remedy?

Half a year later a number of Irish Peers, led as of
old by the Duke of Leinster and Lord Charlemont, followed the example of the Commoners, and petitioned
Parliament to take the condition of Ireland into
immediate consideration. The use of force, though
it might be effective for the suppression of disorder,
could not remove discontent.

Even the English Whigs did not escape the prevailing influence. A party manifesto was published
in the *Edinburgh Review*, revised by Lord John
Russell,* offering among other concessions an annual

* See *Select Correspondence of Macvey Napier*, then editor
of the *Edinburgh Review*.

visit of the Queen, and a residence in Ireland long
enough to make the presence of the Sovereign no
unusual element in national life, the holding of parliamentary sessions in Dublin, a provision for middle-
class education by erecting Maynooth into a university,
reform of land tenure, the disestablishment of the
Protestant Church, and a permanent provision for the
Catholic Clergy, and for the maintenance of their
churches. A sum yielding an annual income of three
hundred thousand pounds must be granted for the
purpose of carrying out these reforms.

A more curious and significant evidence of progress
was an Irish Club started in London. A dozen peers,
more than twenty members of Parliament, as many
baronets, knights, or privy councillors, and a considerable muster of artists and literary men united in
the Irish Society. It was to be independent of
religious and political distinctions, and the names of
men so widely divided as Frederick Shaw, Emerson
Tennent, and Colonel Taylor on one side, and
Anthony Blake, D. R. Pigot, and Thomas Redington
on the other, promised that it would be national in a
high sense. Irish artists like Maclise, MacDowell,
John Doyle, and men of letters like Father Prout and
Dr. Croly, gave it an attraction more piquant than rank
can furnish, and it opened with satisfactory prospects.

The land question was more and more debated in

the *Nation* as the most urgent of Irish grievances, and one for which redress might perhaps be obtained from the Imperial Parliament.

When the monster meetings had arrayed the bulk of the nation on his side, and the time for mere demonstration was over, O'Connell promised that he would summon a Council of Three Hundred to consider the question of international securities, and form the nucleus of an Irish Parliament. The young men took up the project warmly, but not without a secret apprehension that O'Connell meant it to create alarm in England rather than to perform the noble work for which it seemed fit.

The meetings still swelled in numbers, passion, and purpose. O'Connell's oratory kept measure with the quick march of the nation. At Davis's birth-place he used language afterwards known as the "Mallow Defiance," Speaking of a rumour which attributed to the Government the intention of suppressing the movement by force, he said :—

"Do you know, I never felt such a loathing for speechifying as I do at present. The time is coming when we must be doing. Gentlemen, you may learn the alternative to live as slaves or die as freemen. No! you will not be freemen if you be not perfectly in the right and your enemies in the wrong. I think I perceive a fixed disposition on the part of our Saxon traducers to put us to the test. The efforts already made by them have been most abortive and ridiculous. In the midst of peace and tranquillity they are covering our land with troops. Yes, I speak with the awful determination with which I commenced my address, in consequence of news received this day. There was no House of Commons on Thursday, for the Cabinet was considering what they should do, not for Ireland, but against her. But, gentlemen, as long as they leave us a rag of the Constitution we will stand on it. We will violate no law, we will assail no enemy; but you are much mistaken if you think others will not assail you. (A voice—We are ready to meet them.) To be sure you are. Do you think I suppose you to be cowards or fools?"

He put the case that the Union was destructive to England instead of Ireland, and demanded whether Englishmen under such circumstances would not insist on its repeal.

"What are Irishmen," he asked, "that they should be denied an equal privilege? Have we not the ordinary courage of Englishmen? Are we to be called slaves? Are we to be trampled under foot? Oh! they shall never trample me, at least (no, no). I say they may trample me, but it will be my dead body they will trample on, not the living man."

The Repeal Association, to stamp this sentiment on marble, voted a statue of O'Connell as he spoke at Mallow, with the final sentence of his declaration carved on the pedestal, in eternal memory of a great wrong adequately encountered. The statue was duly carved, but meantime O'Connell's policy has rendered the motto impossible.

These transactions excited profound interest throughout the civilized world.   The United States sent back
an answer to them in immense meetings held in the
great cities, at which eminent senators, judges, and
statesmen took part.   England was warned that if she
coerced Ireland, she would do so at the risk of losing
Canada by American arms.   Seward, afterwards
Secretary of State, and John Tyler, then President of
the United States, declared that the Union ought to be
repealed.   One of the great meetings sent an address
to France, inviting her to help a nation which had
helped her on a hundred battlefields.   France answered
by a memorable meeting in Paris, at which deputies
and journalists took part who before four years had
themselves become the Provisional Government of a
new republic.   They offered arms and trained officers
to a country resisting manifest injustice.   In these
transactions it became plain that France and America
recognised as a spokesman of the Irish race, not only
O'Connell but the *Nation*.   The writings of the paper
were spoken of in their correspondence, and quoted
in a hundred newspapers from New York to New
Orleans, and were universally translated by the press
of Paris.   The attendance at the monster meetings
continued to grow, till it was alleged that at Tara little
short of a million of men met to claim self-government for their native country.

CHAPTER V.

THE RECREATIONS OF A PATRIOT. 1843.

MAN'S character is often best read in his amusements. He may pose on the platform, or in the salon, but in holiday undress he needs must follow the bent of his nature. At the very climax of popular agitatation in the autumn of 1843, a meeting of the British Association was fixed to be held at Cork, and Davis, as a native of the county, promised to attend. He proposed at the same time to take a holiday from work, and employ it in an extensive tour in Munster and Connaught, which would enable him to communicate with important political allies, and probably to make new friends for the cause. He needed not merely leisure, but solitude. To be wholly alone at times, disengaged

from the closest friendships and the tenderest domestic
ties, is a necessity to the original and fruitful thinker.

His correspondence during this excursion, with
some help from memoranda which he made at the
moment, enables us to follow him closely. During
the greatest stress of work or travel he was an inces-
sant student, and in his leisure the practice clung to
him. The *Paradise Lost* and the *Transfiguration
of Raphael*, Emerson declares, are results of a note-
book; and Davis has left behind him a bundle of
note-books during his excursions or studies. Unhappily they are often quite undecipherable; or, if
legible, phrases which to him were doubtless symbols
of vivid impressions yield small results to any one else.
They were sometimes written in pencil, and, after
half a century, have faded into shadows. When
pen and ink were employed, he trusted so largely to
his memory that the notes constitute a sort of
memoria technica. He probably felt the truth of the
poet Gray's memorable saying—that half a word set
down at the moment is worth a cart-load of recollections. But, such as they are, they enable us to watch
the student hiving with loving care the materials which
gave local colour and dramatic character to national
ballads, or furnished the statesman with data on which
opinion was founded. He gathered traditions of historic events where they happened, studied the aspect

and topography of memorable places—there are such
studies of Limerick, Galway, Derry, and Drogheda,
for example, with rude maps and drawings of the
battle-fields. Scraps of local songs and vocabularies
of Irish phrases are interrupted to set down the names
of men who might be useful to the national cause or
who were familiar with local antiquities, notes on the
administration of justice in the provinces, drawings
of old coins, or memoranda of articles to be written
by himself or others.

He travelled by Kilkenny, Waterford, and Cashel,
and reported in a letter to his friend Webb the
official business transacted at Cork :—

"The association meeting was successful for its science
both to natives and strangers ; but because the Repealers
and the educated shopkeepers of Cork sustained it, the
county Conservatives declined to join it, so the number
was only six hundred instead of fifteen hundred, as had
been usual. However, we had a thousand at the ball."

In his diary we find his impressions of Dr. Murphy,
the Catholic Bishop, who had collected a great library
which he proposed to bequeath to some public
purpose.

"Dr. Murphy : met me, drove [with him to his]
house ; some middling pictures and prints. 100,000
vols. (catalogue in Feast-book). 6,000 this year, great
in classics and illustrated books. Buys second-hand ;
gives 5 per cent. to dealers ; does not go to auctions
nor order them ; buys much in Belgium ; says that

the convents supplied the great libraries of France and Belgium. The Bishop said—

"'I was dining with Cardinal Gonsalvi when Canova arrived with the rescued pictures and statues from Paris. All rose. Gonsalvi embraced him and saluted him Marquis with a pension of 5,000 crowns a year. He refused. "Oh, his Holiness must not be refused." "Well, I accept it on condition of its being given to poor artists in Rome."'"

He heard from the Bishop and others stories of an eminent sculptor, at that time in Dublin, having recently returned from Rome. John Hogan was originally a carpenter, and by force of native genius raised himself to be one of the greatest artists of his generation in Europe.

"Hogan; 2 [of his] chalk drawings at Macroom; they are in a carpenter's [named Hogan]; H. worked in Mrs. Deane's [as a carpenter] Sir T. D——'s [Sir Thomas Deane, a local architect], mother. After nine month's vain entreaty, Sir T. got him for Dr. Murphy, for Mrs. D. Murphy was then about to fit up the chapel, had the plaster done, and the bracket and canopies and niches ready; he got pictures of the apostles, etc., cut the likeness and drapery, all boldly but loosely. He has 27 wood figures in that sanctuary, a half-relief altar—Leonardi's 'Last Supper,' free, clear, and noble. Carey saw the altar-piece and asked for the carver. He is a carpenter.' 'Bring him hither.' Carey took a hand and a Socrates' head to Dublin Society. They could not, as he was not a pupil, but they gave him 25 guineas for the head and hand, and offered £100 [to start him in an artistic career] if Cork gave another (see their books). Hogan got £300, gave £150 to his family, and started for Rome, with many letters from Dr. M. ; delivered none of them, but bought a block, hired lodgings, shut himself up for six months. [A shepherd boy playing on his pipe was his first success ;] and then an Italian bag-piper was there to play for Rome for ever. He was commissioned to make Dead Christ for Dr. M. He did so, and was allowed by Dr. M. to exhibit and then sell it in Dublin. Clarendon Street Chapel has it, but he did another in Italy. When 'twas opened, after it came from Leghorn, the head was found unfinished. 'Why?' 'I wish to prevent jealous people saying I got Italian help. I shall do this here under their eyes.' (This fine work is now under the high alter in the Carmelite Church, Clarendon Street, Dublin.) Mr. J. Murphy has bust of Dr. M. and himself by H. Dead Christ, large noble man in full health ; drapery round, fine, and true, but at side too heavy stone-lying ; head on right shoulder, right foot over left, elbows on ground, hands on sides, wedged-up head, neck, flesh. A cemetery angel by him, deep, gentle, reflective, wing exquisite."

When he left the city for the county Cork he picked up traditions which, when they were carefully sifted, might furnish materials for history. Nearly every great estate in Munster is the result of some great crime, and he found a notable instance :—

'Beecher's great grandfather came here possessing no-thing. Young O'Driscoll got him to take care of his house while he was abroad with his sister. When he came back Beecher prosecuted him under the Penal Laws (as a Papist) and got his property."

K

"O'Leary shot for outlawry for refusing horse for £5 at Mallow, and Matthew of Thn. on being asked for his 2 fiery chariot horses drove to the Archbishop and read his recantation."

He looked at the landscape with the eye of a soldier and a poet :—

"All these Southern heads have castles and as many are peninsulas; these castles are on the necks—thus securing some 20, or 30, or 50 acres for tillage, cattle, plunder, and stores. There the galleys were beached, doubtless, in winter [when they were not] plundering in more gentle seas. All these O'Heas, O'Donovans' O'Sullivans, Burkes, O'Malleys, O'Loghlens, O'Driscolls, O'Mahonys, etc., were doubtless pirates or sea-kings (see in Waterford Hist.) O'Dll's alliances and invasions, Burke the marine, Grace O'Malley's galleys in 1172, privateers in 1645. Thorpe's pamphlets and coast traditions. [Thorpe's pamphlets are a valuable collection in the Royal Irish Acaademy.]"

"In Tipperary and Kilkenny, grey eyes, black lashes, rich brown hair, middle or small size, oval-faced arch girls; now dark hair, flashing black eyes, brunette, sunny cheeks, bearing graceful. Tela girl lovely horse-woman."

To Pigot he sent a glance at Mount Melleray, the famous Trappist convent in the Waterford mountains.

"The institution consists of a MITRED abbot, the only one in Ireland, one prior, nine other priests, besides religious and lay brothers—in all about seventy. The priests, besides their religious duties, are as teachers in the schools, superintendents of work, etc., and they alone speak—the rest are eternally silent day and night, in and out. They are engaged in tilling their land, and in the trades necessary to their independence. They have five hundred and sixty acres on the mountain, of which over two hundred are under cultivation. They have a fine garden, highly tilled, and a hot-house, with vines, flowers, etc. I send you a geranium blossom of theirs. Until lately they were dependent for many things; now they raise their food (vegetables and milk and butter), grind their corn (wheat and rye), make and mend their own clothes, tools, harness, build their houses, paint and carve pictures and statues for their chapel, and are grooms, carpenters, smiths, foresters, masons, schoolmasters, and wheelwrights. Their school is new, but not bad. Fancy this abbey, with its tall white spire and thriving ascetic unnatural community staring in heaven's face from the side of the great free lordly wild mountain, and you have Mount Melleray. They all wear brown gowns and hoods and brogues, save the priests, who wear white. St. Bernard was their founder, and they have a fine manuscript of the Psalms with music in his writing. I have got a most pressing invitation to go there for some time, and whenever I like."

In Tipperary, on his downward journey, he found traditions of scornful and wicked oppression which have borne bitter fruit in latter times.

"Father F—— says, I remember Sir John Fitz-Gerald bidding all the people in Cashel fair kneel, and they knelt, and he waved his sword over them, walking through them."

"Pierce Meagher's ancestor was at the wake of Lloyd of Meldrun, who was his kindest friend. Jacob of Mewbarn came to young Lloyd, afterwards, with list of

Catholic conspirators. One of them was Meagher, and
the great meeting night was the night of Lloyd's
wake. 'He was at my father's wake that night, and
your informer lies,' says Lloyd. 'Well, we'll leave HIM
out and hang the rest.' 'If you offer to touch one of
them I'll denounce you all.'"

Smith O'Brien's recent proceedings in Parliament
made him a man worth cultivating for public ends ;
and Davis asked Webb to send him an introduction, Webb being a near kinsman of Mrs. O'Brien.
He went to Kerry chiefly to confer with Maurice
O'Connell, whom he believed more disposed to resolute policy than the other members of his family ; and,
doubtless, he was, before domestic troubles drained
his life of all purpose. He loved and honoured Davis
and longed to share his noble aims, but his will was
a bow unbent for ever.

Here are memoranda, probably of the same date,
containing hints for work and study :—

"I feel more and more that a good novel is the
greatest of works, the natural combination of all objects
and natures, whereas other things are selections from
feelings or subjects, and admit of a magnifying with
consistency, as in Shakespeare ; but it, perhaps, would
be impossible to write consistent a superhuman novel
from the multitude of objects. . . .

"The late owner of Castle R——, to preserve it, con-
tracted with a mason to build a wall round it. He did
so with the stones of the castle itself !

"Mr. Hunter states that, in the schools on his own

and Mr. Maxwell's property, the Irish blood is first in the class, as all his female connections inform him."

At Limerick he met the gifted brother of Gerald Griffin, author of *The Collegians*, a novel which has since rivalled the circulation of *Guy Mannering* and *Tom Jones*, and he gathered some facts about that unhappy man of genius.

His correspondence with me during this journey was naturally on the political business transacted in Dublin. The young men saw great possibilities in the project of a Council of Three Hundred, and immediately looked out for constituencies. Davis asked me to find him one, preferably in the North.

"I am slow to write directly on the Three Hundred," he said. "If the people were more educated I would rather postpone it for a year; but they would grow lawless and sceptical, so I fear this cannot be done. If O'Connell would pre-arrange, or allow others to pre-arrange a 'decided' policy, I would look confidently to the Three Hundred as bringing matters to an issue in the best way. As it is, we must try and hit on some medium. We must not postpone it till Parliament meets, for the Three Hundred will not be a sufficiently free and brilliant thing to shine down St. Stephen's and defy its coercion. Yet we must not push it too quickly, as the country, so far as I can see, is not braced up to any emergency. Ours is a tremenduous responsibility, politically and personally, and we must see where we are going."

"I am not neglecting the Three Hundred. 'Grattan's Memoirs' by his son, Hardy's 'Life of Charlemont,'

WALKER'S MAGAZINE (of which there is a copy in the
Association Library) contain materials on Dungannon.
Notice the Catholic Committee of 1792, Wyse, Tone,
Grattan, etc. Tone says 'twas one of the noblest
assemblies he ever saw. Copy the passage. You ought
to print the census sheet I left you, at once, correcting
it by the large volume of the Census which you should
buy and notice, or send to me to notice, and by Captain Larcom's paper read here. By the way, the Repealers had the whole association here. Who wrote
the 'Ways and Means?'* 'Twas excellent. Write to me
soon. . . . You seem to have a turn for genealogy. I wish
you knew my eldest brother, who has the most extraordinary gifts in that way I ever met.   There is no
family in Munster but he knows the pedigree of; but,
alas, he is an English-minded man."

I replied :—

"I have secured your return (and your £100) for
county Down.   Mr. Doran [Rev. John Doran, P.P.,
Loughbrickland] undertakes to manage it all without
further flapping. I did not consult John O'Connell, for
reasons that I will tell you when you return; but if
you prefer Dublin and can secure it, you are not bound
to Down—it only waits your convenience.   I am glad
you intend to do an anniversary article. Do not forget
the influence of our songs, and popular projects, or
the foreign notice the national question obtained through
the NATION, or the universal adoption of its tone by
the provincial press. I meditate a song upon the same
happy occasion.

"Your report was confirmed—the way the cow killed

---

* See *Voice of the Nation,* p. 35, where it is published with the
writer's name.

the hare—by chance. John O'Connell read it to the Committee, or rather in the Committee, for not a soul seemed to be listening, as the great man was telling a story about Watty Cox. When the story and the report were finished I said I would be happy to move the adoption of the latter, if I could hope that anybody knew what it was about; whereupon O'Connell, who has the most extraordinary faculty of knowing what is going on without apparently attending to it, said he quite agreed with me in approving of it, and would second the motion. The work was then, of course, done, and I announced the general fact, assuming that you would go into detail thereafter."*

About the same time he wrote :—

"MacN——'s article [in the NATION] on the Whigs has given great offence in many quarters. I think to say truth, it said too much, and looked like a cruel attack, when the Irish Whigs at least were doing nobly in the House. Take some opportunity to distinguish that you did not mean them (S. O'Brien and the like) in attacking the Whigs, and do not notice anything in the London Press on it. I speak advisedly. We have need of tolerants as well as allies for a while."

Before turning to the west, he wrote to Maddyn :—

"What do the Britishers mean to do with our Three Hundred? What do the longheads think of it? What do you think of it? I am offered several places in it. Ought I to go in? I think 'yes,' from policy and conscience. Pray write to me at length, and very soon."

Maddyn strongly dissuaded him from entering the Council.

* September 27, 1843.

"The Government," he wrote, "will never permit it to assemble. They will put it down, and challenge the country to resist, and all reasonable men of the Whigs, Conservatives, and Moderates will approve of the Government resolution. By the 1st of March, 1844, it will be seen that no man will have lost more reputation than O'Connell, and no man gained more than Peel. I would strongly advise you not to fetter yourself more than you are at present. Do not shackle yourself by assuming responsibilities, while you will not be allowed to retain your own right of decision. . . . All parties here are ready unsparingly to employ force, if you will persist in your resolution to plunge into a bloody civil war. The Irish think Peel is cowed because he holds back and does not obey the counsels of the ultra Tories. 'Twas so with Pitt in 1790, and subsequently. He did not go to war until he saw that it was absolutely necessary; and the moment he gave the word he regained his popularity with the governing public of England. Depend upon it that O'Connell will be defeated in this business."

During this autumn Sir Charles Trevelyan, a Treasury official, who had seen service in India, and, as brother-in-law of Macaulay, had the ear of the Government, visited Ireland to report on the state of public feeling. He disbelieved in O'Connell's sincerity, but he found the bulk of the people determined Nationalists, eager to fight when called upon by their leader, and the Catholic clergy he believed were in complete sympathy with them. But he added:—

"There is another estate in the Repeal organization,

of the existence of which the people of England are imperfectly instructed—the young men of the capital. As far as the difference in the circumstances of the two countries admitted, they answered to the 'jeunes gens de Paris.' They were public-spirited enthusiastic men, possessed (as it seemed to him), of that crude information on political subjects which induced several of the Whig and Conservative leaders to be Radicals in their youth. They supplied all the good writing, the history, the poetry, and the political philosophy, such as it was of the party."

His judgment of O'Connell seemed at the time shamefully unjust. But the private correspondence of O'Connell has since been published, and we find that, after the muster of the nation at Tara, when the soul of the people was on fire for self-government, he addressed a letter to Lord Campbell, the party gladiator who held for a few weeks the office from which Lord Plunket had been driven, recommending measures for conciliating Ireland by concessions, and restoring the Whigs to office.

"Why does not Lord John [Russell] treat us to a magniloquent [? magnificent] epistle declaratory of his determination to abate the Church nuisance in Ireland, to augment our popular franchise, to vivify our new Corporations, to mitigate the statute law as between landlord and tenant, to strike off a few more rotten boroughs in England, and to give the representatives to our great counties? In short, why does he not prove himself a high-minded, high-gifted statesman, capable of leading his friends into all the advantages to be derived from conciliating the Irish nation, and strengthening the British Empire?"*

A better insight into the purpose and hopes of the young men than Sir Charles Trevelyan had attained, will be found in a letter which Davis addressed to the Duke of Wellington, under the signature of a Federalist, debating the pros and cons of coercion and concession :—

"This is not the place to examine whether a country with two thousand miles of coast can be blockaded— whether a territory of thirty-two thousand square miles can be occupied by a man a mile—whether the science of cities would not furnish important supplies to the strong hands of the peasants—whether a country so un-even in surface, so cut up by clay ditches, and cabins, and villages, and little ravines, and inhabited by so many field-workers, could be traversed by squadron or field battery—for these questions I must refer others to Keatinge, Cockburne, Roche Fermoy, the maps, and to the fore-mentioned list of books. I beg your Grace's pardon—I refer them to a higher authority on the military resources of Ireland and on the doctrines of war than any one living or dead—to the Duke of Wellington."

He goes on to tell the Duke the state of opinion among the educated classes, the great factor in all political changes; but paints, it must be confessed, rather his hopes than his experience.

---

* Letter to Lord Campbell, Sept. 9, 1843,

"I heard hints of a diplomacy embracing rich and angry spirits, and extending to more than one state. I heard of a system of retaliation, severe, just, and systematic enough to insure for Irish insurgents what it won for Washington and the American rebels—all the rights of war. The sober organization and the manageable fury of the people were dwelt upon. I heard of field works, and plans for subdividing a mob in a few hours. I heard of an ingenious and formidable commissariat, of American steamers, of Colonial and Chartist insurrections, of friendly foes and leading genius. Most of the Conservatives and many of the Whigs said that an insurrection would occur, and would be suppressed, unless France interfered, either by going to war at once, or by winking at private expeditions, such as went to Greece and Spain. But the rich men among them seem to dread a defeated as much as a successful insurrection. The break-up of trade, the terrible shock to English reputation, and the enormous expenditure which an insurrection would occasion, were not the only grounds of their fear.

"Your lordship will readily understand the connection between the land tenures here, and insurgent hopes. The landlords believe that the first act of an insurgent general would be to proclaim the abolition of rent, and to bid the people 'take the land, and fight hard to keep it.' Such an appeal they speak of with terror. They believe that the thoughtful and adventurous yeomen of Leinster would adhere to a cause so advocated. They think that the Presbyterians, discontented at the tenancies-at-will, to which, in spite of the rules of the Ulster settlement, and of common creed and common right, their tenures are limited, would rise to a man. They fear that the trampled serfs of Connaught would learn hope by vengeance, and courage by example; and they know that the chivalrous peasantry of the South would sweep all before them till some great army was brought on their front, if even that would check their course."

During Davis's tour in Munster the political work of the Association, and the educational work of his colleagues went on vigorously. At Mullaghmast the Nationalists of Leinster assembled in immense numbers. The trades and citizens of Dublin met at Donnybrook, fed on memories of what great cities— Athens and Rome, Bruges and Ghent,—had done for liberty; and the population of the Metropolitan County was summoned to assemble at Clontarf, a memorable battle-field. But a trivial incident arrested the tide of success. The vast troops of horsemen who attended the monster meetings were named Repeal Cavalry in some provincial newspapers; and an indiscreet secretary of the Clontarf meeting, in issuing the programme of proceedings, assigned a place to the "Repeal Cavalry." This political blunder was promptly corrected by order of O'Connell; but the Government, who understood perfectly well that it was the folly of a subordinate, seized on the incident as a pretence for suppressing the meeting. A proclamation was issued forbidding it to assemble, and warning all loyal and peaceful persons from attending.

It is useless to debate in this place what O'Connell

ought to have done to maintain the right of public meeting, or what he might have been expected to do after the specific language of the Mallow defiance. What he did was to protest against the illegality of the proclamation, and submit actively and passively to its orders.   He was the leader, alone commissioned to act with decisive authority, and he warned the people from appearing at the appointed place.   By assiduous exertions of the local clergy and Repeal wardens they were kept away, and a collision with the troops avoided.   But such a termination of a movement so menacing and defiant was a decisive victory for the Government; they promptly improved the occasion by announcing in the *Evening Mail* their intention to arrest O'Connell and a batch of his associates on a charge of conspiring to "excite ill will among her Majesty's subjects, to weaken their confidence in the administration of justice, and to obtain by unlawful methods a change in the constitution and government of the country, and for that purpose to excite disaffection among her Majesty's troops."

Next day, Saturday, the 14th of October, O'Connell, his son John, T. M. Ray, Secretary of the Association; three journalists of the national party, John Gray, Charles Gavan Duffy, and Richard Barrett; and two country priests, Fathers Tyrrell and Tierney, were arrested, but admitted to bail to take their trial for the imputed offence.

When the news of the proclamation reached Davis at Galway, he saw that the supreme crisis of the cause had arrived. He knew that O'Connell was pledged to resist any violation of the right of public meeting till the aggressor passed over his dead body, and he was persuaded that the people at the slightest sign would fly to his assistance. He started straightway for Castlebar to consult John Dillon on ulterior measures, and, as he had papers at Bagot Street which might compromise others, he sent instructions to his mother to burn them. But, when the arrests provoked no resistance, he hurried back to Dublin. When he met his friends we found him painfully discomposed by the retreat before the proclamation.   The gathering confidence of the people in their own strength, their reliance on the professions of their leader, as well as the new desire which Davis had done so much to plant, that their acts might adequately correspond with their words, were all dissipated.   After such an anticlimax it was impossible to believe that a conflict with England, in which the whole nation would be arrayed under the green banner, would take place during the lifetime of O'Connell.

The blow fell heaviest on the young men. In the words of a native chronicler they had brought "a new soul into Eire." They had inflamed their own generation with the noble purpose and desire to endure suffering and sacrifice for their country, a supreme service to a people striving to be free, and now the toil and triumph of a hundred laborious weeks was squandered in a moment.

It is needless to describe in detail how disastrously our dreams were scattered,—

"How toppled down the piles of hope we reared."

It was a time of despondency and misery, of rage, and almost of despair. Davis's first emotion was expressed in mingled wrath and scorn :—

"We must not fail, we must not fail, however fraud or
　　force assail ;
By honour, pride, and policy, by Heaven itself !—we
　　must be free.

"We called the ends of earth to view the gallant deeds
　　we swore to do ;
They knew us wronged, they knew us brave, and, all
　　we asked, they freely gave.

"We promised loud, and boasted high, 'to break our
　　country's chains or die ;'
And should we quail, that country's name will be the
　　synonym of shame.

"Earth is not deep enough to hide the coward slave
　　who shrinks aside ;
Hell is not hot enough to scathe the ruffian wretch who
　　breaks his faith.

"But—calm, my soul !—we promised true her destined
　　work our land shall do ;
Thought, courage, patience will prevail ! we shall not
　　fail—we shall no fail !"

Up to this time Davis's policy might be expressed in the simplest formula. He desired that the passion and purpose of the people should be raised to the scale of 1782, when England would again yield to the will of a united nation, or, if she would not yield, that the Repealers should do what the Volunteers would assuredly have done, fight for the liberty denied to them. When these hopes disappeared, his first thought was to quit the Repeal Association for ever. He would serve Ireland in some other field, for a great purpose is like a great river, dammed at one point it forces its way by some other path towards its unchanging goal.

After repeated conferences, we resolved to accept the situation which O'Connell had created, and turn it to account in preparing for the future. While he lived it was plain nothing could be done, everything might and must be done hereafter. From that time the energy of the young men was employed in projects of education and discipline. Between the arrest of O'Connell and the era of the famine and the French Revolution, the *Nation* swarmed with projects fostering a lofty but not impracticable nationality. The fruition of our hopes was admitted to be distant, but it might be made more sure and more precious by a wise use of the interval.

The arrest of O'Connell was quickly followed by his trial. That transaction can only be glanced at in a memoir of Thomas Davis. It proved a signal consummation of the system of misgovernment on which he made war, and rendered its hidden iniquity intelligible to Europe and America. The Catholic chief of a Catholic nation was tried in a Catholic city before four judges and twelve special jurors among whom there was not a single Catholic. But among the four Irish judges there was an Englishman, and among the twelve Irish jurors there was another of the same race and opinions.

The trial lasted five and twenty days, and at every stage was marked by the infringement of the settled law or established practice governing trials of this nature. At the close the Chief Justice charged for a conviction with what proved to be illegal violence; and a jury of partisans, as carefully selected as the juries which tried the State prisoners of the Stuarts, found a prompt verdict against all the traversers of whom one had only attended a single meeting of the Association and been a member barely five days.[*]

The prosecution brought a great accession of funds and a large body of recruits to the Repeal party. The most notable recruit was William Smith O'Brien. He

---

[*] The story of the trial is told in detail in *Young Ireland,* Book 2nd.

L.

was younger son of a house famous in Irish annals,
since more than a century before the English invasion.
He was a man of good estate, long discipline in Parliament and public life, of active intellect, but, above
all, of universally acknowledged probity and disin-
terestedness. He was received with enthusiasm, and
immediately became by common consent the second
man in the movement.

Between the verdict and the sentence, O'Connell
was urged by Whig friends to visit England, and promised a significant ovation. He might help them to
overturn Peel, and if this could be done promptly, he
would never be called up for judgment. But the
most serious of the National party greatly dreaded the
experiment. O'Connell, as they knew, stood between
two dangers. He was strongly possessed with the
apprehension that Peel would improve his victory by a
Coercion Act, enabling him to suppress the Association and forbid public meetings. And he was surrounded by Whigs of the official class, wooing him
back to the bosom of that party. Immediately after
the verdict he went the length of proposing in committee to dissolve the Repeal Association ; and this
disaster was only averted by the young men declaring
that they could not follow him into a new association if
the existing one was sacrificed to a panic. O'Connell
was made to realise, almost for the first time, that a

new class had grown up about him, who were his faithful and zealous allies, but would never be his servitors or henchmen.

O'Connell went to England, and was rapturously welcomed in the House of Commons by the Whig opposition ; went to an Anti-Corn Law League meeting at Covent Garden Theatre, and was the hero of the occasion ; was invited to public meetings in various large towns in the north, and to a public dinner in London. But what his English sympathisers claimed on his behalf was such justice to Ireland as would supersede Repeal. O'Connell's language before his English audience was not reassuring ; and he alone of all men could sacrifice the National cause. He could no longer induce the people to retreat openly, as in 1834, but he might render success impossible during his lifetime. Davis was deeply pained and alarmed. He wrote a letter to John O'Connell, intended as usual for his father's eyes, and his grief and fear pierce through its courteous and moderated phrases.

"I do not, and cannot suppose that your father ever dreamt of abandoning Repeal to escape a prison, yet that is implied in all the Whig articles. If he had such a purpose, this partial conciliation of Leaguers and demi-Chartists would not accomplish it. Peel, not Sturge, wields the judgment. Nothing but a dissolution of the

Association would, we are directly told, prevent the sentence. To dissolve the Association would be to abdicate his power, and ruin his country.

. . . "Then, why should your father embarrass his future Repeal policy by a sojourn in England, and still more by identifying us with the English as if he were (still) a Precursor and sought to cement the Union, not dissolve it? . . . If this continues we shall have neither a Repeal agitation nor a Liberal Government, whereas a vigorous pursuit of Repeal now would retain the one and give the only chance of the other."

The private correspondence of Davis was rarely more extensive and varied than at this period. He wrote to Maddyn in the interest of a poet whom we all cherished.

"I think you were a reader of the UNIVERSITY MAGA-ZINE. If so, you must have noticed the 'Anthologia Germanica,' 'Leaflets from the German Oak,' 'Oriental Nights,' and other translations, and apparent transla-tions of Clarence Mangan. He has some small salary in the College Library, and has to support himself and his brother. His health is wretched. Charles Duffy is most anxious to have the papers I have described printed in London, for which they are better suited than for Dublin. Now, you will greatly oblige me by asking Newby if he will publish them, giving Mangan £50 for the edition. If he refuse, you can say that Charles Duffy will repay him half the £50 should the work be a failure. Should he still declare against it, pray let me know soon what would be the best way of getting some payment and publication for Mangan's papers. Many of the ballads are Mangan's own, and are first-rate. Were they on Irish subjects he would be paid for them here. They ought to succeed in London nigh as well as the 'Prout Papers.'"

Maddyn doubtless did his best, but he did not succeed, and the greatest poet of his generation lived and died unknown to London publishers. Even in Dublin his poems only got published by one of his friends advancing £50 to James M'Glashen, whose magazine they had enriched.

The *Citizen* on which Davis had spent so much care and pains, which a few months earlier he was ready to prefer to the *Nation* as a national organ, was staggering towards a final fall. In April he wrote to Maddyn :—

"Our poor magazine is really dead at last. The expense had kept increasing, and the sale diminishing, and it was necessary to stop. The amphibious politics of the magazine, the high price, and unequal ability were enough to sink anything. The publishers were careless and without influence, and the perpetual change of size and price most absurd." *

Other educational projects were pushed on vigorously. Davis negotiated successfully between James Duffy, by this time the recognized publisher of the party, and the author's brother, for a uniform edition of the national novels of Gerald Griffin, and for a new edition of Dr. R. R. Madden's *United Irish-*

* 61 Bagot Street, April 13, 1843.

men. And, at the same time, I induced Mr. Duffy to accept a manuscript novel from William Carleton, up to that date a name odious to Catholic booksellers ; and *Valentine McClutchy* marked a new departure in the career of a man of genius. O'Connell's *Memoir of Ireland, Native and Saxon,* had been originally published in America, and the European copyright was presented by the author to O'Neill Daunt, on whom the labour of collecting the materials had chiefly fallen ; and I persuaded James Duffy to purchase it at three hundred pounds—a liberal price for a volume to be published at a couple of shillings. A *Pictorial History of Ireland* consisting of coloured lithographs by Henry MacManus, with short biographical or historical illustrations by O'Callaghan, proved unhappily a failure—the only complete collapse among the projects of the party.

The signs of intellectual success, which were discernible on all sides, have been described elsewhere in language which it will be convenient to borrow :—

"Books upon the history and condition of Ireland were now published in France, Prussia, and Belgium, and portraits of the conspirators were to be found in every town and village between the Atlantic and the Pacific, and in every great city on the continent of Europe. More than a quarter of a century later, when these transactions were nearly forgotten by a new generation in Ireland, I was startled to find for sale under one of the piazzas of Turin a large lithograph designated 'Capi e Promotori della Questione Irelandese'—being no other than the convicted conspirators of 1844.

"The Association, in pursuance of its new policy, offered a prize for the best essay on a Constitution for Ireland, and exhorted competitors to remember that 'the difficulties of the case must not be evaded, but frankly stated, and the means specified by which they might be best met.' The Celtic race, though obstinate in its habits, is very susceptible of discipline; no peasant girl so speedily acquires ease and intelligence by living among the cultivated classes. The enthusiasm of the time which had enabled an entire nation to become water-drinkers would, it is hoped, enable them to submit to other discipline and other sacrifices. It was admirable to see how young men of all ranks entered into this idea. This progress was obvious; but there was progress more important which could not be measured. Davis possessed the rare faculty of exciting impatience of wrong without awakening the deadly hatred of those who profit by it; and it was only in after years men came to know how deeply the new ideas penetrated among cultivated Protestants. Joseph Le Fanu was the literary leader of the young Conservatives, and Isaac Butt their political leader; both were at this time engaged, privately and unknown to each other, in writing historical romances which would present the hereditary feuds of Catholics and Protestants in a juster light to their posterity. Samuel Ferguson, more essentially a man of letters and more indisputably a man of genius than either, broke through the hostile silence of the Dublin University Magazine, by predicting with generous exaggeration that, if no untoward event interrupted their career,

the time would come when the national writers in
Dublin would be read with something of the same enthusiasm in Paris as men in Dublin were reading
Béranger and Lamartine.   Even in Ulster, the home of
prejudice in latter times, they had reason to know that
their songs found favour, and, like Moore's, were heard
in unwonted places.   And in the stronghold of bigotry,
in the office of the EVENING MAIL, at the feet of the
astute parson who directed its politics, there was growing up a lad who in a few years broke away from
hereditary prejudice to become the laureate of Irish
treason." *

Before this time Dillon had ceased to write in the
Nation, except on an occasional spurt; MacNevin
took his place, and gay banter and persiflage succeeded to philosophical speculation and humanized
Benthamism.   But he was not idle; he was a constant critic on his friends, and his lenient and sympathetic strictures sank deep.

Of the *Nation* of this period Davis has written,
" Duffy and I wrote most of the paper; " but he wrote
much more than I did, as the business of administration fell exclusively on me.   A modern editor, sometimes, like the leader of an orchestra, never plays a
bar, but is content to direct the movement and
determine the time of his band.   This was not my
idea of the duties of the position.   I wrote as much

* * Young Ireland*, bk. ii., chap. iv.

as an office permitted which involved a huge correspondence and a constant supervision of whatever was published, that the character of the journal might be guarded as scrupulously as a gentleman guards his personal honour.

The verdict against the State prisoners was not followed, as we have seen, by immediate punishment, the sentence being postponed, according to practice, until the opening of next term. In the interval eminent lawyers at the English and Irish bar pronounced the proceedings to be illegal in essential particulars, and advised an appeal to the House of Lords by writ of error. O'Connell, when he returned from his English expedition, found the people exasperated by the idea of his imprisonment, and attempted to tranquilize opinion by a device which like an accommodation bill, helped to swell his liabilities to an impossible total. " Give me," he said, " but six months of peace, and I will give you my head on a block if we have not a parliament in College Green."

Davis reported to his friend Pigot the state of affairs in Dublin at this period.

"The newspapers will tell you the news. Your Whig friends are wrong. There is, at last, a dogged spirit in this country which will tell in any way we have to use it. The only danger is that 'the sudden news of

O'Connell's imprisonment, which was not expected, may cause some petty rows.

"O'C[onnell] and Duffy are in good health and spirits, and they are the most important [of the Repeal convicts]."

Davis esteemed Wolfe Tone to be the most sagacious Irishman born in the eighteenth century. He projected a union of Catholics and Protestants in the distracted country, and accomplished his design in the United Irishmen. He landed in France without credentials or money, and launched a French expedition against the British power in Ireland, which, like the Armada, failed, only because it was scattered by a hurricane. Tone's name was familiar to students, but, though he had a monument in the United States, there was no memorial of his services in the land for which he died. A few friends at this time subscribed funds to place a tombstone on his grave in Bodenstown cemetery with this inscription written by Davis:—

"THEOBALD WOLFE TONE,
Born 20th June, 1763;
Died 19th November, 1798,
FOR
IRELAND."

On May 30, 1844, the traversers were brought up for judgment. They claimed to stand out till the writ of error was tried by the House of Lords; but they were immediately sentenced to fine and imprisonment, and sent to Richmond Bridewell. The metropolitan prisons were under the control of the Dublin corporation, and by their connivance the imprisonment amounted to mere detention in a country-house with handsome and extensive gardens. The governor and deputy-governor were authorized to let their official residences to the prisoners. We had separate suites of rooms, our own servants, a common table, which was rendered luxurious by gifts of venison, fish, game, and hot-house fruits, and the unrestricted society of our friends. O'Connell proposed to write his memoirs in this retirement, and the journalists worked unrestrictedly at their profession. John O'Connell, who liked to play at journalism, set up a *Richmond Prison Gazette*, consisting chiefly of banter and pasquinades on the prisoners by each other; and we gave audience to sympathisers on fixed days, and had a conference with Smith O'Brien on the business of the Association twice a week.

During the weary progress of the State trial, Davis spoke to me for the first time of a long retirement from the *Nation*. He would travel, he would employ himself in historical or political studies, but he doubted if there was any useful or honourable work for him at Conciliation Hall. These designs, as we shall see, were not altogether relinquished, but his fidelity to

O'Brien and to his more intimate associates, and the necessity which a strong man feels to face the danger nearest at hand kept him at his post, and to do his best while on duty was the practice of his life. He made suggestions to the counsel of the traversers, especially to Whiteside, on the historical defence relied on, which proved of substantial value.

A design which he long cherished was to write a history of Ireland. It was a great want. There was no history which could be put into the hands of a student or an inquirer without shame, and no one was so fit as he for the task. But its chief attraction for him was the escape it would afford him from Conciliation Hall, and his friends, who knew that he would leave a fatal void in the national ranks, discouraged the design. He was engaged in work which was not indeed higher, for a Prescot or a Thierry is one of the greatest gifts Providence could bestow upon Ireland, but was far more urgent. It would have been a bad economy of life to lay down his habitual task, and seclude himself from the interests of the hour, even for such a purpose ; yet this is what he desired to do. In the middle of the State trials he pressed the project on me for the second or third time.

"MY DEAR DUFFY,

"I think it better for me to begin my history at once, and give the next five weeks exclusively to it,

and I can work for the same time in summer for you,
which will transfer the term of our arrangement to the
beginning of July instead of the end of May. I can be
much more useful to you then than now ; and, at any
rate, I know that, as it will convenience me, you will
manage without me for a while.

. . . "I think that, obliged as you are to be in court,
it would be most easy for you to write the State Trial
articles, and that it would prevent your getting idle or
ennuyé at court.   You ought to rise and breakfast at
seven, and take half an hour's run before you go to the
court, and, in fact, resolve to lead a most fresh vigorous
life to sustain you against QUI TAM's speeches [Qui Tam
was a nickname for the Attorney-General]. I'll see you
at court to-morrow."

Some weeks later he returned to the subject :—

"Will you or MacNevin," he wrote to me, "deal
with the Debate? My mother's sister is dying in our
house, and I cannot bring myself to this work.

"And now I want to know could you postpone the
second half of my engagement with the NATION, until
autumn, or entirely? I know this is a very unreasonable request. But I find that I must either give up
the notion of writing the history, or absolutely stop
writing for the NATION during the spring. Would not
the sum you agreed to give me procure a sufficient
variety of other writing to compensate for the absence
of my harum-scarum articles?   But do not decide
hastily. I am in a very sobered mood, and feel doubts,
serious doubts, of my ability to write the history at
all. But I shall speak to you next week of this."

My remonstrance, however, and the intractable
difficulties of the case, induced him to modify his plan

into the project of a history in eras, each era treated by a separate writer. Among his papers I find a note of the latter design :—

"'History of the Pale,'—C. G. D.
"'The Civil Wars,' i.e. from end of Pale to Cromwell's, and the Acts of his Parliament QUOAD Ireland,—T.D.
"'Patriot Parliament,' 1689 to 1792, and from 1792 to 1800,—T. D. ; 1800 to 1844,—D. O. M."

But three men can no more write history to the accompaniment of a State trial than one man. In the end it was determined to begin modestly, and put off the larger design for calmer times. The Committee of the Repeal Association were induced to offer a prize for a school history of Ireland, and I find among his papers a letter discussing this project :—

"I wish you would consider these two suggestions about the proposed history while the notice is still unpublished.
"1. It ought to come down to the Union, and no later. If it come to the present time, you will have odious and lying exaggerations about O'Connell, and, what is worse, injustice to the other men engaged in the Catholic Agitation. Depend upon it there will be no avoiding this, but by stopping the history at the Union. Moreover, proceedings so recent will occupy such an undue share of the book as to crush out more material facts. Let the O'Connell Agitation be glorified in a book published for the special purpose, and written by Dr. Stephen Murphy !

"2. Eight months is obviously too short a period to write a history in. Take an average writer, and he would need three months to collect his materials, three months to arrange and digest them, and, if he wrote the book in three months more it would be at the rate of a hunt. This would be nine months. But as a writer is a man and not a steam engine, you would need to throw in a couple of months for relaxation and his other employments. He may be a farmer (John Keogh's grandson), an attorney (Mitchel), a doctor (Cane), or some other man with his hands full of work, and it is surely more important to have a good book than to have one a few months before the seasonable time. I think you ought to allow a year for a book that you intend to be permanent and standard; but if it is desirable to avoid so long a delay, fix the 1st of March instead of the first of January, 1846. This will only postpone the book two months—nothing to the Association, everything to the writer plunging hopelessly through his last chapters."*

While he still meditated writing the history immediately, he had correspondence with Maddyn and John O'Donovan, the antiquary, which is of permanent interest, though perhaps the latter permits his opinion to be a little too much tainted with jealousy of a rival, and quite inferior, translator from the Gaelic.

O'Donovan wrote to him :—

"Having heard that you are engaged on a history of the English Invasion of Ireland, I beg to say that I am anxious to show you some notes of mine on certain

* Duffy to Davis.

facts connected with this period of Irish history. The
translation of the 'Annals of the Four Masters,' published by Mr. Geraghty, though put into readable
English by Mangan, is full of errors, and you will find
it very unsafe to trust it. . . . I see that Mr. Duffy
has made a slight allusion to the stiffness of my translations from the Gaelic, because I do not know English.
I know English about six times better than I know
Irish, but I have no notion of becoming a forger, like
MacPherson. The translations from Irish by Mangan,
mentioned by Mr. Duffy, are very good;* but how
near are they to the literal translations furnished to
Mangan by Mr. Curry? Are they the shadow of a
shade? Mr. Duffy speaks as if Mangan had translated
directly from the original! But the world is now too
knowing for silly assertions of this kind. . . . , It may
be useful just now to talk of long faded glories; but
it is my opinion that we have but few national glories
to boast of in our history, which only proves that,
though we were vigorous and partially civilized, we
never had any national wisdom. Let me conclude by
one remark, that it is my opinion that the NATION
newspaper, even though it is no child of the tribe of
Dan, has done more to liberalize the Irish and implant
in the minds of the Anglo-Irish and Iberno-English
the seedlings of national union, than all the histories
of Ireland ever written, and that, if it continues to
live as long more as it has already lived, without
flinching from the noble principles it has hitherto maintained, its effects on the national mind will not be
easily removed. I wish I could boast of our having
had such literature in the days of Cormac Mac Art, or
even Brian Boru."

* *Ballad Poetry of Ireland.* The stiff translations alluded
to were Hardiman's, not O'Donovan's.

On a detached sheet of his diary, without date, I found a significant entry, which, as I conjecture, belongs to this period. He had never travelled, and he longed to obtain the practical acquaintance with races and institutions, and with art and political geography, which travel alone supplies. It was only at this period of his short public life that he could have withdrawn himself from his engagements for six months, and he still feared that there would be a long interval of timid and wavering counsels at Conciliation Hall, when he would be best employed in training himself for the future.

"Write for NATION till August, then Scotland and Norway for two months (£50), Hamburg, Prussia, Munich, Austria, Venice, Switzerland, Paris, Turin, Italy, Spain, and home; £250 or £300 in all. Or go in June to Scotland, Hamburg, Berlin, Munich, Vienna, Trieste, Venice, Switzerland; in all, three months: then September and half October in France, half October, November, and half December in Italy, home for Christmas: in all, six months. Good! Morning letters to Dillon and Duffy."

But the imprisonment opened an era and an opportunity which put these dreams to flight.

CHAPTER VI.

THE STATESMAN. 1844.

'CONNELL and a half dozen selected agitators were locked up in Richmond bridewell, and now the critical question arose, Could the agitation live without the agitators? It is a strange craze of English politicians to believe that discontent in Ireland depends upon the action of this man or that, instead of springing perennially from the condition of the people. It is a power which may be regulated and disciplined, indeed, but it is no more created by human skill than one of the unintermittent forces of nature. It was now about to become more vigilant and formidable, more patient and determined after defeat, than it had been at the height of the monster meetings.

The new leader, Smith O'Brien, was a man of good

capacity, careful training, and large experience in public affairs. His manners were a little rigid and formal, and his utterance too deliberate for Celtic taste, but his generous heart kept him young and fresh. He was ready to compete with his juniors in labour and to surpass them in sacrifice. As a scion of a great historic house descended from King Brian, the Alfred of Ireland, and a member of Parliament of unstained probity and recognised success, he occupied a unique position. He was not only the greatest recruit the cause had won, but he created the hope of a decisive movement among the class to which he belonged. O'Connell had proclaimed him his personal representative, and the mouthpiece of the national cause during the imprisonment; and O'Brien devoted every faculty of his being to the task imposed upon him. He loved to be surrounded by men of probity and capacity, and had no jealousy of their gifts. He had large belief and confidence in Davis, who speedily came to bear the same relation to him that Alexander Hamilton bore to Washington. He formulated the policy of the official chief, supplemented his projects with kindred proposals of his own, and clothed their common purpose in the persuasive language of genius. O'Brien visited O'Connell and the State prisoners almost daily, consulted them on his plans that nothing might be done which had not the assent of the imprisoned leader, but his own character, and that of Thomas Davis, were soon broadly stamped on the national movement.

Davis for the first time had a free field for his policy, and a direct control of public affairs, and we are able to judge of his gifts as a statesman. There was no more thought of travel or retirement; no more despondency: like a vigorous young tribune called from the ranks of Opposition to be a Minister of State, he began to act and direct like one who had found his proper work, and his influence was soon felt in every province of public affairs. His policy was ready for the hour and for the generation. He had lived in solitude with the great thinkers, and was accustomed to note the currents and undercurrents which control opinion, to note the forces at work to-day, and to foresee the forces which would be at work to-morrow.

A parliamentary committee, organized by O'Brien during the State trial, now completed a series of reports dealing with the main branches of the national question in an exact and practical manner, like men who might soon be called upon to exercise the functions of a national Government. Somewhat later, O'Brien discovered that these political studies had excited interest among a class usually cold and sceptical— the gentlemen who sit on both sides of the Speaker's chair.

"I find," he wrote to Davis, "that our reports have
produced in the minds of the English members an
extraordinary effect, and that my notion of making the
Repeal Association an introductory legislature has been
completely realized. Every intelligent M.P. says that
they are calm, able, and most useful."

As agencies for local action, Repeal Reading Rooms
were multiplied. There were already three hundred :
it was determined to increase them to three thousand ;
and they were directed to contest every elective office
in the interest of Repeal, with candidates of the best
character and capacity obtainable. Though the main
agency relied upon was education, it was not merely
the education of books, but still more the education of
action and responsibility. To plant opinion and create
habits, is to form men, but discipline in public duties
alone can form citizens ; and corporations, boards of
guardians, public schools, and colleges, if occupied by
men of public spirit, might help—

> "To gather up the fragments of our State,
> And in its cold, dismembered body breathe
> The living soul of empire."

Davis rarely spoke in the Association, but his friends
O'Brien, Dillon, MacNevin, Barry, and O'Gorman
were often in the tribune, and gave a tone of confidence to debate, to which it had been a stranger of
late. The Repeal members were summoned to attend

the weekly meetings at Conciliation Hall, and the leading Repealers in the provinces came up in batches for the same purpose, carrying addresses to the State prisoners. Preparations were begun for a general election, and candidates of honour and capacity, fit to be the spokesmen of a nation, were sought for. What sort of representatives the new men wanted was not left in doubt. The existing members had been elected before the country was awakened on the national question, and were for the most part despicable in character and capacity. As missionaries of a subject nation to a dominant one, they were like Lascars sent to convert Brahmins. Davis, in lieu of speaking in Conciliation Hall, wrote on the subject in the *Nation* with admirable frankness :—

"If our members were a majority in the House," he said, "it might not be very moral, but at least it would have some show of excuse, if we sent in a flock of pledged delegates to vote Repeal, regardless of their powers or principles; though even then we might find it hard to get rid of the scoundrels after Repeal was carried, and when Ireland would need virtuous and unremitting wisdom to make her prosper. . . . We want men who are not spendthrifts, drunkards, swindlers,—we want honest men—men whom we would trust with our private money or our family's honour; and sooner than see faded aristocrats and brawling profligates shelter themselves from their honest debtors by a Repeal membership, we would leave Tories and

Whigs undisturbed in their seats, and strive to carry
Repeal by other measures."*

The tone of strict and haughty discipline, designed
to make the people fit to use and fit to enjoy liberty,
was illustrated in the method of dealing with a public
riot at this time.

"We have heard with surprise and anger that a
house in Kilkenny, belonging to one of the jurors in
the State Trials, has been wrecked.

"Such an outrage is an outrage against law, which
we hope and believe the law will sharply punish.

"It is much worse—it is a direct violation of the
principles of the agitation—it is a gross breach of
Repeal discipline—it is a crime against Ireland.

"If a soldier, no matter from what motive, rushes
from his rank in battle, he is, very properly sabred
or shot instantly. If we had the men who perpetrated
this outrage before us, and a clear field, we should
just as unhesitatingly cut them down.

"If we are to carry Repeal—if this is not to be
another of these damnable failures that have disgraced
our intellect and our character—there must not be one
other popular crime. The Irish people deserve to
rot in slavish poverty if they will not keep the discipline under which they are enlisted."

And he taught the rationale of this rigid discipline
in language of transparent plainness :—

"We are not men who bid the people to expect
Repeal in the change from leaf to fruit in any year.

* *Nation*, June 29, 1844.

We have never said it was certain. It is not certain; for if the people do not persevere with a dogged and daily labour for knowledge and independence they will be slaves for generations. It is not at hand, for the Protestants must be in our array, or foreign war must humble our foe; Ireland must be united, or our oppressor in danger, ere we can succeed by moral force; but we ask those who require knowledge, discipline, and civic wisdom as guarantees for our fitness for nationality—Has not Ireland done something to solve their doubts and satisfy their demands?"

Like Swift, he sought to arrest the ear of the Protestant democracy by associating their party tunes with generous and patriotic sentiments.

"'Fruitful our soil where honest men starve;
    Empty the mart, and shipless the bay;
Out of our want the Oligarchs carve;
    Foreigners fatten on our decay!
            Disunited,
            Therefore blighted,
    Ruined and rent by the Englishman's sway;
            Party and creed
            For once have agreed—
Orange and Green will carry the day!
            Boyne's old water,
            Red with slaughter!
Now is as pure as an infant at play;
            So, in our souls,
            Its history rolls,
And Orange and Green will carry the day!"

One of the hardest tasks an Irish leader could attempt was to teach his countrymen to respect the law in a country where the law was so often an instrument of torture, but Davis did not shrink from the attempt, for he knew that deference for authority is an essential basis of good citizenship, and that France had tossed in unrest for a century because she remembered too exclusively the abuses of a power shamefully misused.

"It has been our fondest aim," he wrote at this time, "to shelter the administration of the law from suspicion. Coarse, and criminal, and crude as it is, we had rather see it observed in the sincerity of a delusive confidence in its integrity, than see wronged men loose themselves from its obligations, and take vengeance into their own hands, or weak men bowing to it with slavish fear."

To complete the records of public duties which Davis taught, it will be necessary to cite here language which he employed somewhat later to rebuke agrarian crime in the South, language in which the sternness of an indignant judge is mitigated by the passionate tenderness of a father who sees his children misled to their ruin.

"The people of Munster are in want—will murder feed them? Is there some prolific virtue in the blood of a landlord that the fields of the south will yield a richer crop where it has flowed? Shame, shame, and horror! Oh, to think that these hands, hard with innocent toil, should be reddened with assassination!

Oh, bitter, bitter grief, that the loving breasts of Munster should pillow heads wherein are black plots, and visions of butchery, and shadows of remorse! Oh, woe unutterable, if the men who abandoned the sin of drunkenness should companion with the devil of murder; and if the men who last year vowed patience, order, and virtue, rashly and impiously revel in crime!

"But what do we say? Where are we led by our fears? Surely Munster is against these atrocities—they are the sins of a few—the people are pure and sound, and all will be well with Ireland. 'Tis so, 'tis so; we pray God 'tis so; but yet the people are not without blame!"

The new policy did not long escape notice. Some of the best informed of the English journals pronounced that the agitation had become far more formidable and menacing than in its boisterous days, for it was now sincere and practical, and the extremest of the Orange journals at home declared that the moderation of the leaders was a cover for the worst purposes.

Tait's Magazine was at that time the chief organ of cultured Radicalism in Great Britain, and its editor was among the first to recognise the change. Two months after the imprisonment had commenced, he published this remarkable estimate of the reorganised movement :—

"In Ireland, agitation goes on with a quiet, self-assured strength, that seems remarkably independent of extraneous excitement. The old English notion—

we suspect still the prevalent one—of Irish patriots and
agitators, as being a herd of boastful and frothy
rhetoricians, is now ludicrously false. They are most
careful and earnest men of business. They rejoice in
their strength, but it is with fear and trembling. With
the exulting consciousness of power that men must feel
who hold in their hands the allegiance, and sway the
volition of a nation, they seem to live in perpetual
dread of making a false move. In their own words,
'There is THE DEMON OF REPEATED FAILURE casting his
shadow by us as we move on;' and they are determined, once for all, to exorcise this same demon out
of their country's history. The rumours of a Whig
accession, to be followed by a gracious and merciful
liberation of the Liberator, made them quite nervous;
THAT would be a difficulty, indeed: yet they think
they could get through it. Even the decision on the
writ of error is anticipated, by these impracticable and
hard-headed patriots, with much less of eager excitement than one would suppose. We repeat the expression of our conviction, that the state of Ireland is formidable and menacing, to a degree far beyond what
public opinion in Great Britain has yet realized to
itself."

But though there was a new policy and new
leaders, it was a change of cabinet, not of dynasty,
which had taken place. Business was conducted in
the name and with the sanction of the imprisoned
chief, and his position in the confidence and affection
of his race was carefully maintained.

The *Nation*, which I continued to edit without
interruption in prison, seconded the new policy

con amore. The high prerogative law of the Queen's
Bench was repudiated or ignored. On the week the
imprisonment commenced the journal was printed
with green ink, to express hope and confidence; the
articles which had been pronounced seditious were
republished in a litttle volume entitled *The Voice
of the Nation,* and the prosecuted verse in a new
and costly edition of *The Spirit of the Nation.*

"You have imprisoned three newspaper proprietors,"
Richard Sheil exclaimed in Parliament, "and the Irish
Press is as bold and as exciting as it was before.
Eleven thousand copies of the NATION newspaper
circulate every week through the country, and
administer the strongest provocation to the most enthusiastic spirit of nationality which the highest eloquence in writing can supply."*

Among the sympathisers with O'Connell in prison,
the Whig journals were conspicuous. If a change
of Government took place, they insisted that the
victims of a packed jury and a partizan judge should

---

* The *Nation* was then price sixpence, and eleven thousand
of a circulation which will appear small in the age of penny
papers, represented £550, which the people paid weekly for the
pleasure of reading it—sometimes more than the Repeal rent.

Davis, who set slight value on what is called fame, used to say
that, if he had his will, the songs of the *Nation* would be remembered in after times, and the authors quite forgotten, or
survive only in a legend attributing them to some O'Neill or
McCarthy, whose existence critics would naturally dispute. But
the age of myths ended when the printing-press was set up.

be immediately released. But what some of us feared most—not without reason as it proved in the end—was a renewal of confidential relations between O'Connell and a Liberal Government. It was not thirty months since he had been their submissive ally in Parliament, and the chief controller of their Irish patronage, and a renewal of these relations must be fatal to the national cause.

The new policy of the Association was not too welcome at head-quarters. O'Connell, like both the Bonapartes, was determined to found a dynasty at all costs ; and his second son, his destined successor, was already known among his parasites as the " Young Liberator." That he had none of the essential gifts of a tribune did not quench his ambition, and he dreaded the rise of men who would be unlikely to accept a lay figure as a national leader. To him the best-informed writers agree in attributing troubles which now began to appear. It was the practice of the Association that no resolution should be proposed which had not been previously submitted to the general committee, but Daniel, the cadet of the O'Connells, a young man whose share in public affairs consisted in the task of reading at Conciliation Hall a weekly bulletin from his father in prison, proposed, without previous consultation with the committee, a vote of thanks to the most discreditable and untrustworthy of the Irish members, for a speech in which he had assailed, in violent language, the leaders of the Irish Federalists. Davis was deeply moved, less by the dangerous breach of discipline than by a deliberate reversal of the policy of the Association regarding the Federalists taken with the assent of O'Connell. He wrote to O'Brien who was in the country at the moment :—

"When you write to Richmond notice the fact that Mr. O'Connell's son moved a vote of thanks to Mr. Dillon Browne without the consent of the committee, and did so because of Mr. Browne's opposition to the Charities Bill, which in its present form a majority of the committee approved. What is worse he did so after Mr. Browne had made a speech adverse to our whole policy, attacking the Federalists, calling on the people to turn them out, and this because they did not aid his opposition to a useful measure. I have made up my mind if such conduct be repeated to withdraw silently from the Association. . . . There are higher things than politics, and I never will sacrifice my self-respect to them."

When sentence on the State prisoners was pronounced, notice, as we have seen, was given of a writ of error before the House of Lords, and when the prisoners were nearly three months in Richmond, a day was fixed for taking into consideration the question whether they were legally convicted. This ap-

peal excited but languid interest in Ireland, justice
from such a Court seeming altogether hopeless.

When the writ came to be heard, Lord Lyndhurst
(Lord Chancellor) and his friend Lord Brougham sustained the judgment of the Irish Court, but Lord Cot-
tenham (the Whig Ex-Chancellor), Lord Denman,
and Lord Campbell (Whig Law Lords) reversed it,
with grave censure of the Irish Chief Justice and the
system of jury-packing which he had upheld.

O'Connell's victory over the Government gave the
national cause an immense impetus. It was a great
opportunity, but he was in a condition of mind and
body when opportunities come in vain. Physically
he was in the preliminary stage of a mortal disease,
and morally he had fallen under the influence of his
incapable son, and thought only how best to retreat
from a position which he considered untenable.

At the first meeting Davis produced a pamphlet in
favour of a Federal Union, just published by Mr.
Grey Porter, the High Sheriff of the peculiarly Protestant county of Fermanagh, himself the grandson of
a bishop. Henry Grattan proposed Captain Mockler,
the representative of a noted Orange family, as a
member; and Smith O'Brien announced the adhesion of Hely Hutchinson, brother of the Earl of
Donoughmore. O'Connell's speech, however, was
what men awaited with strained attention, as the

hands of the barometer which announces the coming
weather. It predicted uncertain times. He noticed
in succession various pleas for advancing the
cause, only to reject them; and reserved his favour
for the preposterous design of appealing to the
English constituencies, to require their members
in the House of Commons (where Irish nationality
was in a minority of about two in the hundred), to im-
peach the Government for misfeasance in the late
State trial, before the supreme tribunal of the House
of Lords, where our cause had not so much as one
solitary representative. It is scarcely necessary to
add that impeachment was a process as obsolete as
trial by combat. He talked in private of letting the
Federalists show their hand, and, after a few feeble
speeches in public, retired to Darrynane to take his
annual holiday. At the same time, O'Brien, who had
been overworked during the three months of the imprisonment, went to his country seat, for a short
recess, and John O'Connell reigned at Conciliation
Hall.

Davis urged me also to make holiday after my
temporary imprisonment, and volunteered to
take charge of the *Nation* during my absence. If
rest be the legitimate requittal of work, he had more
claim to a holiday than any of us, but he would not
hear of beginning it till after my return.

I had accepted an invitation from O'Connell, to visit him in his mountain home in Kerry; two of my frends, John O'Hagan and D. F. McCarthy, accompanied me, and there are frequent allusions to this excursion in Davis's letters at this time. To Pigot he wrote :—

"O'C. expects you to Darrynane. You will meet Duffy, etc., there, and would greatly like it. . . Hudson is in Wales, and sent me a trumpet call, a quick step, and an air from it. Also an essay on the language which, after all, he seems to think is Celtic. Hurrah for my ancestors, and for yours, and you, and myself, and, as poor Tone I think says, hurrah generally."*

After three weeks spent among the noble scenery of Waterford, Cork, and Kerry, as we approached Darrynane, I announced to Davis my intention of returning immediately to town, and setting him free for an autumn excursion, but he declined the proposal.

"MY DEAR D.—You MUST not come back here till the middle of October. I cannot leave town, as one of my brothers is going to be married about the middle of next month. I will then go to Belfast to meet Thomas O'Hagan. The NATION is easy to me, and will grow easier. Send 'Laurence O'Toole' within a week, or leave it to number six [of the revised 'Spirit of the Nation']. I am proud of my own dear, dear Munster, having pleased you so much. I love it almost

* 67 Bagot Street, September 29, 1844.

N

to tears at the thought.   I wrote to William Griffin
[brother of Gerald Griffin, author of the 'Collegians'],
he will gladly guide you [in Limerick].   Tell McCarthy
to write words to McCarthy's march in the CITIZEN.
Give him my respects, and my best regards to John
O'Hagan. E. B. Roche* wants much to meet you and
to get you to Trabolgan.

"Tell O'Connell that the first news Robert Tighe [an
Irish barrister] had of the liberation was from the
shouting of the Frankfort mob!   What other man
since Napoleon could have produced such an effect?
Present my respects to the O'Connells, and believe me
as busy as a swallow."

O'Connell, in his pleasant home fast by the Atlantic,
was a patriarchal chief.   His talk was of rural sports
for the most part, and the duties of a country gentleman.†

The object of the northern journey, where Davis
proposed to meet Thomas O'Hagan, was one of grave
import. Mr. O'Hagan had joined the Repeal Association as a Federalist, and many of the more liberal
and enlightened Whigs came to share his belief that
Federation would furnish a solution of the national
difficulty. Sharman Crawford openly declared for it,
and Mr. Ross, the member for Belfast, Colonel Caulfield, brother of the Earl of Charlemont, Mr. Thomas

---

* Then M.P. for Cork County, afterwards Lord Fermoy.
† The visit to Darrynane is described in *Young Ireland*,
book iii., chapter 2.

Hutton, formerly member for Dublin city, and a number of barristers of good standing in their profession, were in general ageement with him. It was proposed to hold a private consultation at Belfast, the cradle of the greatest national movements in the last century. Hudson and Davis, who were ready to go all lengths for unmitigated nationality, promoted this conference, and would have accepted Federalism, and given it a fair trial. There was no public muster-roll of the party, but a memorandum found among Davis's manuscripts indicates how widely he believed the desire for a Federal Union had spread.

"The wealthiest citizens of Dublin, Cork, and Belfast, many of the leading Whig gentry and barristers, and not a few Conservatives of rank, hold Federalist opinions. They include Episcopalians, Presbyterians, Roman Catholics, Repealers and Anti-Repealers."

The theory of the party was that the Union had been effected by corruption and force, that it had worked ruinously for Ireland, and that a new international treaty with juster provisions ought to be substituted for it.

CHAPTER VII.

CONFLICTS WITH O'CONNELL.
1845.

HE best thing that could befall O'Connell after his imprisonment was that the Liberal party should take up Federalism. It would increase prodigiously the chance of a speedy settlement, whether on his lines or theirs. He strove to persuade Crawford and others that their proper course was to join the Association, not as Repealers but as Federalists, as Mr. O'Hagan and the Bishop of Killaloe had done; but they would not listen to this proposal. Some of them disliked and distrusted him personally, and they all knew that no one could induce a tithe of the party to enter Conciliation Hall on any pretence. But the objection to his scheme lay deeper; if the proposal was to be listened to in England, and accepted as an alternative to Repeal, was plain that it must not originate with the Repealers. When it became certain that the Federalists would not join him, O'Connell was seized with the fatal idea of joining them, by declaring himself a convert to their opinions. He had left prison with the determination of retreating definitely from the position of the Mallow defiance, and here, unfortunately, he perceived a favourable opportunity. He privately urged two Federalists who were among his personal friends, William Murphy, a Smithfield salesman of great wealth, and Thomas O'Hagan, to ascertain the wishes and intentions of their political associates. They tried doubtless to comply with his wishes, but without much success. His impatience overcame him, and, while the Belfast consultation was in progress he wrote a letter to the Association announcing this change of opinion. In the midst of a long political disquisition there was this pregnant sentence :—

"For my own part," he said, "I will own that since I have come to contemplate the specific differences, such as they are, between simple Repeal and Federalism, I do at present feel a preference for the Federative plan, as tending more to the utility of Ireland and the maintenance of the connection with England than the proposal of simple Repeal. But I must either deliberately propose or deliberately adopt from some other person a plan of Federative Union before I bind myself to the opinion I now entertain."

The Duke of Wellington's conversion to Catholic Emancipation, Peel's to Free Trade, Disraeli's to Household Suffrage, or Lord John Russell's to religious intolerance in 1851, did not take his party by more complete surprise than this startling declaration. The time was when it would have been received without criticism in the press, as it was actually received in the Association, or with only a subterranean murmur of dissent, but that time was passed. It was felt instinctively that this sudden surrender might be fatal to the national cause by killing popular confidence, and that even as a stroke of policy it was a mistake. If there had not been a national movement strong and triumphant, Federalism would never have been heard of; if the national movement was transformed into Federalism the existing party would probably disappear, for Sharman Crawford and his friends would never serve under O'Connell. Davis was at Belfast, Dillon in Mayo, and all the men with whom I was accustomed to consult gone on their autumn holiday. The course the *Nation* would take was of supreme importance, for if *it* was silent no national journal in the island could be counted on to face the wrath of O'Connell. But Davis was actually engaged in Federal negotiations at the moment, and to denounce Federalism in the *Nation* would be to put him in a false position. On the other hand, to acquiesce after the people had been pledged in twenty monster meetings to unlimited nationality would shame us before our allies in America and France, and humiliate us before our opponents in England, and would infallibly drive the best men out of an Association which did not know its own mind on the most momentous question. It was not Federalism that was objectionable, but putting the livery of the Federal party on the shoulders of Nationalists.

I solved the difficulty by writing as the leading article in the *Nation* a letter to O'Connell in my own name, and speaking only for myself. I objected to the change he proposed, contending that it would not serve Federalism and might ruin Repeal, and insisting courteously that the Association had no more right to alter the constitution upon which its members were recruited than the Irish Parliament had to surrender its own functions without consulting its constituents. The letter was reproduced extensively by the newspapers, and the controversy spread to nearly every journal in the empire, and finally to those of France and the United States. It was generally predicted that the *Nation* and the party it immediately represented would be destroyed, but that, though O'Connell would conquer them, his new profession of faith might be regarded as the funeral oration of Repeal. Neither prediction was verified, both the *Nation* and the public cause outlived the difficulty. The story has been told in detail elsewhere,* and we have to do with it here only as it concerns Thomas Davis.

I wrote to Davis describing the stress of circumstances under which I had acted and inviting him if he agreed with me, to take part in the controversy. He replied :—

"Monaghan, Thursday morning.

"MY DEAR D.—On reflecting that other events may have happened since I left, and regarding the policy of pressing the discussion further at this moment as doubtful, I have concluded not to write on our relations to Federalism, and to ask you to weigh the propriety of letting it be for a week. I shall be in town on the 1st."

During the week's truce of silence which I adopted on Davis's suggestion, O'Connell's personal enemies in the press yelled forth that the Young Irelanders were manifestly conquered in the first skirmish ; were dumb, and swallowed their leek in silence, and so forth.

Davis returned to town immediately, and associated himself with the course taken by the *Nation*.

"We shall rejoice," he wrote, "at the progress of the Federalists, because they advocate national principles and local government. Compared with Unionists

See *Young Ireland*, book iii., chap. 3.

they deserve our warm support; but not an inch further shall we go; principle and policy alike forbid it. Let who will taunt and succumb, we will hold our course. No anti-Irish organ shall stimulate us into a quarrel with any national party; no popular man or influence shall carry us into a compromise. Let the Federalists be an independent and respected party; the Repealers an unbroken league—our stand is with the latter."

And on my own behalf I declared, in relation to the storm of menace with which we were assailed,—

"The legitimate leader of the movement was not more willing to lead than we to follow; we proclaimed strict obedience and discipline as essential to success, and we practised them; for where there are many captains the ship sinks. But at all times, and now not less than any other time, we stood prepared to hold our own opinion against him upon a vital question (such as the present) as freely as against the meanest man of the party. We do not run all risks with a hostile Government, in proclaiming day by day weighty and dangerous truths, to abandon the same right under any other apprehension."

The Federal cause, Davis assumed, was completely ruined by this unexpected *coup* of the leader. To O'Brien, he wrote :—

"All chance of a Federal movement is gone at present, and mainly because of O'Connell's public and private letters; yet I am still doing all in my power to procure it, for I wish to cover O'Connell's retreat.

He is too closely bound up with Ireland for me ever
to feel less than the deepest concern for his welfare
and reputation."*

The Federalists were naturally discouraged and
angry. "O'Connell," said Deasy, " has jumped into
our boat and swamped it." Sharman Crawford was
deeply indignant, and complained privately to O'Brien
that O'Connell had first attempted to wheedle the
Federalists, and then betrayed them.

"He wants," he said, referring to a former transaction,—"he wants to take the same undignified
course, humbugging both Repealers and Federalists;
trying to make the Repealers believe they are Federalists and the Federalists that they are Repealers; and
keeping a joint delusive agitation, knowing right well
that whenever particulars came to be discussed they
would split up like a rope of sand."

But he had inflicted a worse injury on himself than
on any one else. The tone of the national press and
of conspicuous Nationalists was so hostile to his new
opinions that he had to renounce them with something
like contempt. While he still lingered in the country,
he began to note painful evidence that his old popularity had received a painful check. At the beginning
of November he wrote privately to the Secretary of
the O'Connell Tribute :—

* Davis to Smith O'Brien.

"Do you know that I have a feeling of despondency creeping over me on the subject of this year's tribute. It seems almost to have dropped still-born from the Press. In former years, when the announcement appeared it was immediately followed by crowded advertisements in the Dublin papers to meet and arrange the collection. The Cork, Waterford, Limerick, etc., newspapers followed, but there is not one spark alight."*

Doheny, who encountered him at a public dinner at Limerick, on his way to town, thought he was ruffled by the temper of his audience, and he arrived in Dublin in no pleasant mood.†

He returned to the Association at the end of November, and broke contemptuously with the allies he had so recently sought.

"They were bound," he said, "to declare their plan, and he had conjectured that there was something advantageous in it, but he did not go any further; he expressly said he would not bind himself to any plan. Yet a cry was raised, a shout was sent forth,

---

* O'Connell to P. V. Fitzpatrick, Nov. 2, 1844, *Private Correspondence of O'Connell.*

† "Your name was received with the loudest cheers; to such a degree indeed as, in my mind, to rouse the great man's wrath. But although the reception was most flattering, still there is a strong feeling that the *Nation* was wrong in intimating that Dan had abandoned the cause. To be sure most men who entertain that feeling have not inquired into the justice or the value of the argument in the *Nation:* they content themselves with saying that it is necessary to preserve the inviolability of his character " (Doheny to Duffy).

by men who doubtless thought themselves fitter to be
leaders than he was, and several young gentlemen began
to exclaim against him instead of reading his letter for
explanation. It was not that they read his letter and
made a mistake, but they made the mistake and did
not read the letter. He had expected the assistance
of the Federalists, and opened the door as wide as he
could without letting out Irish liberty. But," he continued, "let me tell you a secret :—Federalism is not
worth that"—snapping his fingers. "Federalists, I am
told, are still talking and meeting—much good may it
do them; I wish them all manner of happiness : but
I don't expect any good from it. I saw a little trickery
on the part of their 'aide-de-camp,' but I don't care
for that; I have a great respect for them. I wish
them well. Let them work as well as they can, but
they are none of my children; I have nothing to do
with them."

The risk of the Association being suddenly transformed was at an end, but his northern allies were
disgusted and alienated, and cynical politicians declared
that the punishment of the *Nation* was only postponed
to a favourable opportunity.

The press of all parties made itself busy with the
controversy and its abrupt conclusion. *Tait's Magazine* summed up the situation in terms which represented adequately the verdict of independent spectators :—

"The Agitator has ceased to be master of the agitation. The magician is impotent to exorcise—has only

a qualified and conditional power to command—the spirit that his spells have evoked. He cannot now do what he will with his own; there is a power in the Repeal Association, behind the chair, and greater than the chair. Why did Mr. O'Connell take the first opportunity he could find to snap his fingers at Federalism, so soon after having deliberately and elaborately avowed a preference for it? Not merely because Federalists stood aloof, and did not seem to feel flattered by his preference, but chiefly because Mr. Duffy wrote a certain letter in the NATION—a letter, we may say in passing, which more than confirms the sense we have long entertained of this gentleman's, and his coadjutors' talent, sincerity, and mental independence—refusing, in pretty flat terms, to be marched to or through the Coventry of Federalism. Mr. O'Connell has since, not in the best taste or feeling, sneered at 'the young gentlemen who thought themselves fitter leaders than he was; but the young gentlemen carried the day nevertheless, against the old gentleman. We see in this, that there is a limit to the supremacy of this extraordinary man over the movement which his own genius originated; what he has done he is quite unable to undo; Repeal has a life of its own, independent of his influence or control; his leadership is gladly accepted and submitted to, but always under condition, that he leads the right way."

The punishment of the *Nation* was indeed only postponed. I have heard an experienced statesman declare that the hardest penalties he suffered in public life were penalties for doing some manifest duty, and the young men were destined to pay for their success

in this unsought contest by a long conflict with
O'Connell, which proved disastrous to them, and in
the end fatal to him.

We have seen what Davis and his comrades were
doing for the Irish cause, and how forbearing was their
judgment of O'Connell. They had won a right to his
absolute confidence, and the generous interpretation
which confidence begets; but strong men are rarely
magnanimous, and political leaders, like kings, come to
regard independence as incipient treason. There is
now no doubt that the leader determined to break with
the young men, and, if he could not reduce them to
unquestioning submission, to reduce them at any rate
to political impotence. Paragraphs began to appear
in provincial papers charging Davis with anti-Catholic
sentiments. They might as reasonably have charged
him with anti-Irish prejudices. He was a Protestant
with the most generous and considerate indulgence
for the opinions of the bulk of his countrymen. But
it was a point on which the people were naturally
sensitive and ready to take alarm. The first name
which came to light in connection with this detraction
was a singularly unexpected one. Edward Walsh, a
National schoolmaster, contributed some sweet simple
ballads to the *Nation*, and having afterwards fallen
under the censure of the Board of Education and got
dismissed, supposed that his connection with the

Nation had done him a disservice. I accepted this view of the situation, and obtained other employment for him from Mr. Coffey, proprietor of the *Monitor*. The close work of a newspaper office galled him, and Davis, who sympathised with the poet harnessed to unaccustomed work, got him transferred to the staff of Conciliation Hall, and after a little time procured for him shorter hours and better pay. These circumstances naturally increased our surprise on reading, in a country paper, a letter from Mr. Walsh, stating that Davis, during my absence on the excursion to Darrynane, had rejected one of his poems on account of the Catholic sentiments it contained.* Making the largest allowance for the susceptibility of the poetic temperament, this imputation was little short of an act of baseness, for nothing can be more certain than that such a motive did not operate at all.

In a memoir of Walsh published in the *Celt*, and afterwards attributed, I do not know on what authority, to Charles Kickham, Walsh's unaccountable prejudice against Davis is noted.

"He (Walsh) was proud of Gavan Duffy's friendship and often alluded to it in his correspondence. But the instinct, if we may call it so, by which he allowed himself to be guided in his likings and his antipathies, did assuredly mislead him, in one remarkable instance.

* The letter appeared in the *Wexford Independent*.

When we come to mention the name of the man who
was disliked by Edward Walsh, the reader will receive
the announcement with profound astonishment.   To
us, at all events, it is utterly incomprehensible. . ,
THE MAN whom Edward Walsh disliked was Thomas
Davis ! "

An attack of a much graver character came from
another quarter.   The *Dublin Review*, in noticing
Maddyn's *Ireland and its Rulers*, pointed out that the
assailant of O'Connell was a man who had once been
a Catholic but had abandoned his creed for a more
prosperous one, and it treated the criticism of such a
person with contempt.   The reviewer was a professor
of dogmatic theology, writing in a religious periodical,
and no one will wonder that he insisted on this view of
the transaction.   But Davis, who was jealous for his
friend, and still more for religious liberty, censured the
spirit of the reviewer as destructive of Irish union.

"If this be, as it seems, a threat, all we can say is,
it shall be met.   The Repeal Association, under O'Connell's advice, censured most severely those in Cork
who hissed a convert to Protestantism.   Neither he
nor we nor any of our party will stand tamely by and
see any man threatened or struck by hand or word
for holding or changing his creed.   If this were allowed
(we say it in warning), events would ensue that would
indeed change the destinies of Ireland."

The reviewer, who was a strong passionate, but
perfectly honourable man, turned fiercely on his

critic, and, in a letter to the *Weekly Register*,* denounced the *Nation* as teaching anti-Catholic doctrines. Several instances were cited which it was perfectly possible for a teacher of dogmatic theology to consider dangerous, but which were innocent in design, and if they appeared in any Irish journal of to-day would not attract the slightest censure. The reviewer would have scorned to make any charge which he did not believe to be substantially true, but he was in a passion, and he was fighting for his individual will as vehemently as for his convictions.

These events gave a convenient text to Mr. John O'Connell, and we found after a little time that it was circulated among the priests south and north, that there was a dangerous spirit in the *Nation*, hostile to religion. It is needless to give any answer at present to these accusations. The writers of the *Nation* have lived their lives and for the most part died their deaths, and the question is disposed of on the best evidence. But it is certain that a serious impression was produced at the moment, and carefully worked up by the industry of the "Young Liberator" with at least the tacit sanction of his father. Davis was seriously moved by the fear that, after all that had been done and

---

* The *Weekly Register* (which had outlived the *Morning Register* of which it was an offshoot). He wrote under the signature of "An Irish Priest."

suffered, the national cause might be again ruined by bigotry and hypocrisy. He was still in Ulster when the letters of " An Irish Priest " were published, and he wrote to me from Belfast :—

"I have written to J. O'Connell, O'Brien, etc., by this post, to stop the lies of the bigot journals. I have done so, less even on account of the NATION (which can be steered out of the difficulty in three weeks without any concession), than to ascertain whether the Catholics can and will prevent bigots from interfering with religious liberty. If they cannot, or will not, I shall withdraw from politics; as I am determined not to be the tool of a Catholic ascendancy, while apparently the enemy of British domination. . . . The last NATION is excellent, and is another proof that, after March next, you will be able to let me retreat for a year on my history. I have given up verses since I left Dublin, and feel as if I could not write them again; so leave plenty (for publication in the NATION) when you are going to London. I shall be up by the end of the week. Hudson and I took a sly trip through Monaghan, Leitrim, Roscommon, etc. I am tolerably well in body, and in good spirits."

On the same day he wrote to Smith O'Brien in the same spirit. O'Brien's reply exhibits the just and considerate character of the man. He put himself in the place of his opponents in the controversy, and suggested how much they might urge in support of their views :—

"In compliance with your request," he said, "I have written to O'Connell requesting his intervention to put

a stop to the discussions arising amongst the national
party. I have read the letter of 'An Irish Priest.' It
is very clever, very Catholic, and, if unity were not
essential, it would be a fair manifestation of opinion
adverse to those promulgated by the NATION. I need
not say I agree much more with the opinions of the
writer in the NATION than with those of the Irish
Priest; but, then, you and I should remember that
we are Protestants, and that the bulk of the Irish are
Catholics. I foresee, however, that unless O'Connell
is able and willing to act as a mediator on the present
occasion, we shall have a PRIEST and an ANTI-PRIEST
party among the Catholics of Ireland. This I should
much deplore. Unity is essential to our success, and
therefore division at present would be madness; but
even if Repeal were won, I should deeply regret such
encroachments on the part of the clergy as would
justify organized resistance, or, what is quite as bad,
infidel hostility to all those feelings and opinions upon
which religion rests."

I wrote a specific reply to the Irish Priest in the
journal where his letter had appeared,* and Davis,

* As respects the journal publishing the imputation, I reminded the editor that there was not one of us now charged with
anti-Catholic designs who had not frequently written in his own
paper, before the *Nation* came into existence, and I invited him
to account for the metamorphoses we must have undergone, if
the imputation were well founded, in passing from Elephant
Lane to D'Olier Street. As regards Davis, whose very name
was unknown to the bulk of the National party at that time, I
said, "I am ashamed that any Catholic should make a defence
necessary in the case of a Protestant who, I believe in my soul,
has done more for the nationality of Ireland than any man living
but O'Connell—a man whose labours are traceable through all
the counsels and all the publications of the Association, and in a
new and healthy influence on the art and literature of the country."

who maintained friendly relations with the proprietor since his brief connection with the *Register*, remonstrated with him personally on the injury he was inflicting on the public cause.

John O'Connell replied to Davis's remonstrances in vague generalities, with a significant allusion to the Federal controversy; but his father joined issue in an able and trenchant letter, which treated the remonstrance with scorn, thinly veiled in irony.

"Darrynane, October 30, 1844.

"MY DEAR DAVIS,

"My son John has given me to read your Protestant philippic from Belfast. I have undertaken to answer it, because your writing to my son seems to bespeak a foregone conclusion in your mind, that we are in some way connected with the attacks upon the NATION. Now I most solemnly declare that you are most entirely mistaken—none of us has the slightest inclination to do anything that could in any wise injure that paper or its estimable proprietor, and certainly we are not directly or indirectly implicated in the attacks upon it

"With respect to the 'Italian Censorship,' the NATION ought to be at the fullest liberty to abuse it; and, as regards the 'State Trial Miracle,' the NATION should be at liberty to abuse, not only that, but every other miracle, from the days of the Apostles to the present.

. . . "With respect to the DUBLIN REVIEW, the word 'insolence' appears to me to be totally inapplicable. All the REVIEW did (and I have examined it again

deliberately) was to insist that a man who, from being
a Catholic, became a Protestant, was not a faith-
worthy witness in his attacks upon the Catholic clergy.
Now, independent of that man's religion, of which I
care nothing, there never lived a more odious or disgusting public writer, with one single exception, and
that is the passage in which he praises you.

. . . "I hate bigotry of every kind—Catholic, Protestant, or Dissent—but I do not think there is any
room for my interfering by any public declaration at
present. I cannot join in the exaltation of Presbyterian
purity or brightness of faith; at the same time that
I assert for everybody a perfect right to praise both the
one and the other, liable to be assailed in argument
by those who choose to enter into the controversy at
the other side.   But, with respect to the DUBLIN
REVIEW, I am perfectly convinced the NATION was in
the wrong. However, I take no part either one way
or the other in the subject. As to my using my influence
to prevent this newspaper war, I have no such influence that I could bring to bear. You really can much
better influence the continuence or termination of this
bye-battle than I can. All I am anxious about is the
property in the NATION; I am most anxious that it
should be a lucrative and profitable concern. My desire is to promote its prosperity in every way I could.
I am, besides, proud as an Irishman of the talent displayed in it, and by no one more than by yourself.
It is really an honour to the country, and if you would
lessen a little of your Protestant zeal, and not be angry
when you 'play at bowls in meeting rubbers,' I should
hope that, this skirmish being at an end, the writers
for the NATION will continue their soul-stirring spirit-
enlivening strains, and will continue to 'pioneer the
way' to genuine liberty, to perfect liberality, and
entire political equality for all religious persuasions.

. . . "I beg of you, my dear Davis, to believe, as you may do with the fullest confidence, that I am most sincerely,

"Your attached friend,
"DANIEL O'CONNELL."

Some of the Protestant repealers shared Davis's apprehension. Hely Hutchinson remonstrated with Maurice O'Connell on the danger to the cause, and Burke Roche threatened, a little too boisterously, perhaps, the measures of defence he meditated.

"If I hear much more of this damned outlandish bigotry in Conciliation Hall," he wrote, "I will go over and give you all a piece of my mind, which will be more useful than palatable."*

While Davis was thinking only of the public cause, his associates were thinking of him. He was right, and grandly and heroically right, and they would stand by him whoever might be his assailants. He must not be singled out or isolated; they were all his comrades, and it was a common cause. The prevailing sentiment was not alarm but bitter indignation. It seemed to them manifest perfidy to the cause to assail the man who had served it with most conspicuous genius and a patient assiduity and self-negation without parallel. O'Connell was receiving a princely income from the people; his son was candi-

* Burke Roche to Duffy.

date for the succession to the popular tribunate; but Davis sought or accepted no reward for his labours, beyond the scanty income of a journalist, and was unwilling that his name should be ever heard in public places or seen in the newspapers.

MacNevin was among the first to give expression to this feeling. In a letter to a Belfast newspaper he vindicated his friend.

"Woe," he said, "to the country wherein could be found a single tongue to slander so pure and earnest a man; one whose indomitable labour, whose wonderful information and enthusiasm are devoted, without one thought of ambition or self, to the ardous task of raising up our country."

Davis had friends, MacNevin declared, who would not suffer him to be sacrificed. They repudiated the somewhat fantastic name of "Young Ireland" which had been bestowed upon them, but they admitted and proclaimed the fact of their friendship and union They were members for the most part of the professions, or artists or writers, of competent means and liberal education; and a habit of consulting together and of meeting in social intercourse gave them the appearance of a party, without any desire or design on their part. Why were these men suddenly assailed in national journals? Were they tainted in morals, dishonest in their dealings with the world, or disreput-

able in their conduct? A charge had never been made against any man supposed to belong to their obnoxious school of any crime, vice, immorality, or dishonesty, and they might at least ask that unblemished lives and unimpeached honour should raise the prejudice in their favour of strong religious convictions.

"And what was there that was new and fresh in the agitation in which this party did not participate—nay, I fear not to say it, which they did not devise and originate? Their object was, not to supersede the wholesome excitement of public meetings—the ancient and venerable routine of prescriptive agitation,—but to add to the stimulant of public talking the quiet teaching of the press, the instruction to be derived from books, the more refined excitement of bold and vigorous poetry. Their songs are sung in Protestant drawing-rooms, and their poets have received the unbought approval of the greatest critics in England—poets, let me add with pride, in some instances members of the Catholic priesthood whose teaching we are slanderously represented to disregard, and whose character and sacred profession we are, with audacious falsehood, said to despise."

Character, he said in conclusion, was dear to all honourable men, and, as it was all the reward they sought, they would not permit it to be filched away in silence or with impunity.

The systematic design to defame Davis produced

a reaction which first taught the young men their power. Hitherto they had never aimed at any other result than to work silently in the national cause. They were not popular in the sense of being familiar and favourite names with the people, for to win popularity there must be much self-display and self-assertion, and most of them shrunk from exhibiting themselves. Davis's position in the Irish movement was not unlike Alexander Hamilton's in the American Revolution, and Dillon was in some points akin to Franklin. How obscure these founders of the United States were in their day beside Patrick Henry or Thomas Jefferson, yet without Franklin and Hamilton the revolution would have probably been abortive.

Frederick Lucas, who in the present controversy and in many which succeeded it, sympathised with Conciliation Hall rather than with them, estimated the position of the young men fairly and liberally.

"They have been rapidly rising," he said, "into notice, and into power. They are indeed subordinate to O'Connell, but they openly avow that they belong to another school of doctrine; they have grown up under the shadow of his wings. They have fought cheerfully and loyally under his banners; and, so far as we can judge, they have never exhibited any symptom of a mean, stupid, or illiberal jealousy of his extraordinary and overwhelming authority. But, though they have displayed this free-will docility,

'this proud submission,' 'this dignified obedience,' they
have never concealed the fact that they have marked
out a clear and distinct course for themselves; that
they are not the mere echoes of Mr. O'Connell's sentiments; that they are not the slaves or the servants
of any man."

While this controversy was still running its course it
was checked by a counter-current. It became known
that the English Government, which had long maintained occult relations with the Court of Rome, had
recently sent a gentleman of an old English Catholic
family to the Pope to induce him to forbid Catholic
bishops taking part in the Repeal movement. A letter
had arrived from the Propaganda bearing this character,
and the question how it would be received was
anxiously debated among Protestant Nationalists. The
jealousy of foreign interference, which Irishmen have
always felt and still feel, burst out like a volcano. All
sections of the National party, O'Connell, the Young
Irelanders, and the National Whigs took a decided
stand against any interference by Rome in our secular
affairs.

Other events ensued which made any open attack
on the young men impossible at the moment. Grey
Porter joined the Association on the specific condition
that its accounts should be audited and published,
which hitherto had never been done. Lord Cloncurry,

who could not be induced to enter Conciliation Hall, justified the hopes of the founders of the 'Eighty-two Club by becoming a member. Neither of them would have remained a moment if the bigotry privately fomented made itself heard on the platform. The Dublin Library, an old popular institution, elected the principal Young Irelanders* and some of their friends on its managing committee, and Davis was admitted a member of the Royal Irish Academy. The work done and influenced by the young men at the time made it a dangerous as well as a wicked folly to disparage them.

O'Brien made a point that Davis should take the chair at Conciliation Hall, and a little later moved a vote of thanks to him for his valuable reports, constituting the best part of the work done by the Parliamentary Committee.

A still more momentous transaction diverted attention from these personal troubles. At the opening of the Parliamentary session of 1845, Sir Robert Peel declared that he desired to make peace with Ireland before engaging in a contest with America, which seemed imminent. There was a dangerous conspiracy in Ireland against the authority of Parlia-

---

* Davis, MacNevin, John O'Hagan, Richard O'Gorman, Gavan Duffy, and their friends Smith O'Brien and Sir Colman O'Loghlen, were among the number.

ment which could not be broken up by force ; but he was persuaded that it might be broken up by a spirit of forbearance and generosity. And he was about to make the experiment forthwith.

His first proposal was to increase the grant to Maynooth College, and make it a permanent appropriation, instead of a vote on the estimates, which provoked an annual faction fight. The Maynooth Bill was fiercely resisted in England as "an endowment of Popery;" there was a stormy protest in the House of Commons, and a hurricane of petitions from the country. In Ireland the Nationalists received it thankfully, but the party who were in tranquil possession of a profusely endowed Church and a wealthy University opposed it tooth and nail.

Peel's second proposal was to found an adequate system of middle-class education, which was so profoundly needed in Ireland. Colleges would be established in Cork, Belfast, and Galway, liberally endowed by the State to provide a purely secular education. To this scheme the bulk of the Liberal Irish members, led on this question by Thomas Wyse, gave a cordial welcome. A majority of the Catholic bishops approved of the general design, objecting to certain ill-considered details. All the barristers and country gentlemen in the Association, and the middle-class generally, supported it. To Davis it was like the unhoped-for realization of a dream. To educate the young men of the middle class and of both races, and to educate them together that prejudice and bigotry might be killed in the bud, was one of the projects nearest to his heart. It would strengthen the soul of Ireland with knowledge, he said, and knit the creeds in liberal and trusting friendship. He threw all the vigour of his nature into the task of getting this measure unanimously and thankfully accepted. The plan needed amendment in essential points, but those who designed it would not, it might be safely assumed, permit it to be spoilt for want of reasonable amendments. The students were to be non-resident, and there was not adequate security provided for their good conduct and moral discipline out of class. The appointment of professors was retained in the hands of Government — a method which tended to destroy academic independence. But if these defects were removed, the colleges would be an inestimable gain.

The first note of dissension came from the marplot of the National party. Mr. John O'Connell, in the committee of the Association, denounced the measure as a plot against the faith and morals of the Irish people. This criticism would have been treated with contempt but that his father unexpectedly came to his assistance. O'Connell during his public life had repeatedly advocated the education of our young men in

mixed schools and colleges for the same motives which
influenced Davis, but he now renounced this opinion
as unexpectedly as he had renounced Nationality in
favour of Federalism a few months before, and, echo-
ing the language of a Tory bigot in the House of
Commons, declared the measure to be a huge scheme
of godless education.   Davis besought him to keep the
question out of the Association, whose sole object was
to repeal the Union, and where angry debate was sure
to follow on such a collateral question.   This truce
O'Connell positively declined, and at the first meeting
in Conciliation Hall he proclaimed his fierce antipathy
to the scheme.   Davis immediately followed him,
analysing and vindicating the plan.   O'Connell interposed to declare that debate was premature, as they
had not seen the measure.   Next day a renewed attempt to keep the question out of the Association was
made.   A memorial, signed by forty members of the
general committee, was privately presented to O'Connell supporting this proposal.   The remonstrance was
so formidable that he felt compelled to acquiesce.   It
was agreed that the question should be mentioned no
more in the Association till the bishops had decided,
but both parties were to be at liberty to push their
opinions outside Conciliation Hall.   Davis and all the
writers of the *Nation* appealed successively to the
people, and O'Connell wrote a series of leading articles

in the *Freeman's Journal* to refute them. These proceedings were within the legitimate conditions of the truce, but Mr. John O'Connell considered himself at liberty to use the agency of the Association to send to the country for signature petitions praying for the utter rejection of the Bill. Among the men of mark in the movement there was not so much as one who sided with the O'Connells. But the men of no mark, " the parasites and pickers up of crumbs," were very busy stimulating resistance. And John O'Connell, who had recently represented the Young Irelanders as indifferent to religion, found here a lucky opportunity of insisting that his suspicions were well 'founded. But his sagacious father began to discover a fact he had little suspected, that with the Young Irelanders had grown up a new class of politicians as different from his ordinary retinue as teetotalers were from sots.

The meeting of the Catholic bishops resulted in a memorial to the Lord Lieutenant, professing their "readiness to co-operate with the Government on fair and reasonable terms, in establishing a system for the further extension of academical education," but not in the proposal as it stood, which they considered dangerous to faith and morals. The terms they proposed seem to me to fall within these lines, being essentially just and reasonable. They asked that a fair proportion of the professors and other office-bearers in the colleges should be Catholics, whose moral conduct had been certified by testimonials from their respective prelates; that all appointments to office should be made by a board of trustees, of which the Catholic bishops of the province where the college was erected should be members; that any officer convicted before the board of attempting to undermine the faith or injure the morals of any student should immediately be removed from office by the board; that as the students were to be non-resident, there should be a chaplain appointed to superintend the moral and religious instruction of the Catholic students, to be appointed on the recommendation of the bishop of the diocese in which the college was situated, who should also have the power of removing him.

There was another concession demanded which might have been made the subject of a compromise. The bishops pointed out that Catholic students could not attend lectures on history, metaphysics, moral philosophy, geology, or anatomy, as they were taught by Protestant professors, without imminent danger to their faith and morals. But history might have been omitted from the course; it is best studied in the closet: and Protestants, it was suggested, would not object to anatomy or geology being taught by Catholic professors. But O'Connell was determined

there should be no agreement.   He would defeat the
Young Irelanders where they had put forth all their
strength ; and it may be further surmised that he was
determined Peel should not rob his late allies, the
Whigs, of the credit of conciliating Ireland.   At the
meeting following the publication of the bishops'
memorial, he declared that they had pronounced the
nefarious scheme dangerous to faith and morals, and
affirmed that it must be rejected utterly.   Let there
be separate colleges in separate cities, for Catholics,
Protestants, and Presbyterians, and no education in
common.   Mr. John O'Connell followed, exaggerating
the opinions of his father, and denying that the
bishops sanctioned mixed education.   Smith O'Brien
declared that he honoured the solicitude of Catholics
for religious education, but he himself thought a
system of adequate precaution might be engrafted on
the Government scheme.

Among Davis's fellow-students in college was a
young man named Michael George Conway.   He was
gifted with prompt speech and unblushing effrontery.
But he wanted conduct and integrity, and had
gradually fallen out of men's esteem.   He had been
recently blackballed, by the Young Irelanders he
believed, in the 'Eighty-two Club, and he came down
to the Association burning for revenge.   He fell on
a chance phrase of Barry's in the debate, misrepre-

P

sented it outrageously, and declared that it was characteristic of his party and his principles—a party on which the strong hand of O'Connell must be laid.

"The sentiment triumphant in the meeting that day was a sentiment common to all Ireland. The Calvinist or Episcopalian of the North, the Unitarian, the Sectaries, every man who had any faith in Christianity was resolved that it should neither be robbed nor thieved by a faction half acquainted with the principles they put forward, and not at all comprehending the Irish character or the Irish heart. Were his audience prepared to yield up old discord or sympathies to the theories of Young Ireland? As a Catholic and as an Irishman, while he was ready to meet his Protestant friends upon an equal platform, he would resent any attempt at ascendancy, whether it came from honest Protestants or honest professing Catholics."

During the delivery of this false and intemperate harangue O'Connell cheered every offensive sentence, and finally took off his cap and waved it over his head triumphantly. He knew, as all the intelligent spectators knew, that a man destitute of character and veracity was libelling men as pure and disinterested as any who had ever served a public cause, and he took part with the scoundrel. It was one of the weaknesses of his public life to prefer agents who dared not resist his will ; but this open preference of evil to good was the most unlucky stroke of his life. Twelve months later he died, having in the meantime lost his prodigious popularity and power; and of all the circumstances which produced that tragic result, the most operative was probably his conduct during this day.

Davis followed Mr. Conway. The feeling uppermost in his mind was probably suggested by the contrast between the life of the man and his new heroic opinions; and it will help to put the reader in the same standpoint if I inform him that the pious Mr. Conway a few years later professed himself a convert to Protestantism to obtain the wages of a proselytizing society.

The reader knows in some degree what Thomas Davis was, what were his life and services, what his relations to his Catholic countrymen were; that he had left hereditary friends and kith and kin to act with O'Connell for Irish ends; and they may estimate the effect which the attempt to represent him as a bigot had upon the generous and upright among his audience. Dillon ruptured a small blood vessel (as we shall see later) with restrained wrath; others broke for ever the tie which had bound them to O'Connell. He was not worthy, they declared, of the service of men of honour, who used weapons so vile against a man of unquestioned honour.

Davis took up the question of the colleges, and

examined it with undisturbed temper and judgment.
He did not regard himself as a debater, but he
proved on this occasion to be a master of debate.
Cool, resolute, good humoured, he raised and disposed
of point after point with unbroken suavity, in a manner
I have never heard exceeded in legislatures or party
counsels.

" 'I have not,' Davis said on rising, 'more than a
few words to say in reply to the useful, judicious, and
spirited speech of my old college friend, my Catholic
friend, my very Catholic friend, Mr. Conway.'

" Mr. O'Connell: 'It is no crime to be a Catholic,
I hope.'

" Mr. Davis: 'No, surely no, for—'

" Mr. O'Connell: 'The sneer with which you used
the word would lead to the inference.'

" Mr. Davis: 'No, sir; no. My best friends, my
nearest friends, my truest friends, are Catholics.   I
was brought up in a mixed seminary, where I learned
to know, and, knowing, to love my countrymen, a love
that shall not be disturbed by these casual and unhappy
dissensions.   Disunion, alas! destroyed our country for
centuries.   Men of Ireland, shall it destroy it again?' "

While he spoke O'Connell, who sat near him, distracted him by constant observations in an undertone;
but the young man proceeded with unruffled de-
meanour and calm mastery of his subject. He cordially approved of the memorial of the Catholic bishops,
which declared for mixed education with certain

necessary precautions. They asked for "a fair proportion" of the professors, meaning beyond dispute,
that the remainder should be Protestants—this was
mixed instruction. They demanded that, in certain
specified branches, Catholic students should be taught
by Catholic professors—this was a just demand, but it
implied a system of mixed education. He like them
objected to the Bill as containing no provision for the
religious discipline of the boys taken away from the
paternal shelter; and, beyond all, he denounced it
for giving the Government a right to appoint and dismiss professors—which was a right to corrupt and in-
timidate.

O'Connell, who had already spoken for two hours,
made a second speech in reply to Davis. His pero-
ration was a memorable one. The venerated hierarchy, he insisted, had condemned the principle of
the Bill as dangerous to the faith and morals of the
Catholic people.

"But," he said in conclusion, "the principle of the
bill has been supported by Mr. Davis, and was advocated in a newspaper professing to be the organ of the
Roman Catholic people of this country, but which I
emphatically pronounce to be no such thing. The
sections of politicians styling themselves the Young Ireland Party, anxious to rule the destinies of this country,
start up and support this measure. There is no such party
as that styled 'Young Ireland.' There may be a few
individuals who take that denomination on themselves.

I am for Old Ireland. 'Tis time that this delusion should
be put an end to.   'Young Ireland' may play what
pranks they please.   I do not envy them the name
they rejoice in.   I shall stand by Old Ireland; and I
have some slight notion that Old Ireland will stand by
me."

I have elsewhere described the scene which ensued.*

"When O'Connell sat down consternation was universal; he had commenced a war in which either by
success or failure he would bring ruin on the national
cause.   Smith O'Brien and Henry Grattan, who were
sitting near him, probably remonstrated, for in a few
minutes he rose again to withdraw the nickname of
'Young Ireland,' as he understood it was disclaimed by
those to whom it was applied.   Davis immediately re-
joined that he was glad to get rid of the assumption
that there were factions in the Association.   He never
knew any other feeling among his friends, except in
the momentary heat of passion, but that they were
bound to work together for Irish nationality.   They
were bound, among other motives, by a strong affection
towards Daniel O'Connell; a feeling which he himself
had habitually expressed in his private correspondence
with his dearest and closest friends.

"At this point the strong self-restrained man paused
from emotion, and broke into irrepresible tears.   He was
habitually neither emotional nor demonstrative, but he
had been in a state of nervous anxiety for hours; the
cause for which he had laboured so long and sacrificed
so much was in peril on both hands.   The Association
might be broken up by a conflict with O'Connell, or
it might endure a worse fate if it became despicable by

* *Young Ireland*, book iii., chap 7, "The Provincial Colleges."

suppressing convictions of public duty at his dictation.
With these fears were mixed the recollection of the
generous forbearance from blame and the promptitude
to praise which marked his own relations to O'Connell,
and the painful contrast with these sentiments presented
by the scene he had just witnessed. He shed tears
from the strong passion of a strong man. The leaders
of the Commons of England, the venerable Coke, John
Pym, and Sir John Eliot, men of iron will, wept when
Charles I. extinguished the hope of an understanding
between the people and the Crown. Tears of wounded
sensibility choked the utterance of Fox when Burke
publically renounced his friendship. Both the public
and the private motives united to assail the sensibility
of Davis.

"O'Connell, whose instincts were generous and cordial, and who was only suspicious from training and
violent by set purpose, immediately interposed with
warm expressions of good will. He had never felt
more gratified than by this evidence of regard. If
Mr. Davis were overcome, it overcame him also; he
thanked him cordially, and tendered him his hand.
The Association applauded their reconciliation with enthusiasm."

Davis's friends were too angry at the injustice he had
suffered to sympathise with his generous emotion,
and some of them remonstrated in private. But he
was determined to make nothing of the incident so
far as it concerned himself. He wrote to Pigot :—

"I send you the FREEMAN of to-day, by which you'll
see that O'Connell and I came to a blow-up in the

Association, but were reconciled, and fancy ourselves better friends than ever. I hope so."

"I am delighted to tell you that John Dillon is better, and Corrigan thinks he can travel to the country at once. On Monday night he had an alarming effusion of blood in the lungs, and consumption was feared. He had been subject to coughs all the winter used to sit in hot rooms, drink quantities of coarse tea, and take little exercise. His chest is now relieved, his voice strong, and his spirits up, but he must take the greatest care of himself and live healthily. The excitement of Monday (for he was sitting behind me when I had the row with O'C.) seems to have caused the rupture, and as he has got over it, the alarm may be useful."

He wrote in the same spirit to Denny Lane. Lane's reply will enable a judicious reader to comprehend the motive-power of the party—the desire to serve Ireland at whatever disadvantage, and the total absence of personal aims. There were considerations, he said, which must never be lost sight of.

"The first is that O'Connell is the most popular man that ever lived, and will be implicitly obeyed by a great body of the people whatever be the orders he gives them. Next, he is so used to implicit obedience, and has so often been able to get on after having cast off those who mutinied against his nod, that he will think nothing of doing the same again. . . . Next, the man is so thoroughly Irish and hearty, and so devoted to the religion to which the people are devoted, that he is, without exaggeration, loved by them as a father. Next, the Catholics are bound to him by their gratitude for his achievement of Emancipation, and nine-tenths of the priests throughout Ireland are his servants and the people's masters. Well, what does all this come to? To this, that his power is irresistible, and that the power of the people of Ireland is rendered ten times more effective than it would otherwise be, being concentrated in his person, so that, even if it could, it should not be resisted unless in extremities. Next, he does not bear control; you can give him no more than a hint of differing in opinion from him. If you have power, and differ from him you cause a split and do serious mischief. Suppose you have no power besides your own, if you differ from him he cuts you off and destroys your usefulness to the cause. Division has been our bane, and is to be avoided by every means short of dishonour, or great or irreparable injury to the cause; if it becomes absolutely necessary to differ from O'Connell, you must get O'Brien, who is a sensible man, and will do so only in an extreme case, to express in the most temperate manner your dissent. O'Connell would never have dared to treat him as he treated you. . . . I have more to say to you, but I am afraid you are tired already. I will write to you again to-morrow about the display here. Show this letter to Barry, and also, if you like, to Duffy."

But Lane did not know, none of us knew, that O'Connell had by this time made up his mind to let the national question fall into abeyance, and to renew his alliance with the Whigs.

Davis was not turned aside a moment from his task. He prepared a petition asking amendments in the

Bill, which was signed by leading citizens of Dublin, the flower of the Liberal bar, and every man of weight or character connected with the Repeal Association outside O'Connell's family. It was determined in the committee of the Association that the Irish members should attend Parliament for a short time, and strive to effect amendments in the Bill. Sir Robert Peel held out hopes that he would modify the method of appointing professors, and he promised to add clauses facilitating the endownment by private benevolence of divinity lectures and the erection of halls for their delivery. He was eager to make the measure a practical success, but he had the bigotry of England in revolt against him, and O'Connell whom he was accustomed to regard as the legitimate spokesman of Irish opinion, showed no disposition to be contented with any amendments. O'Connell wrote repeatedly private notes to the Archbishop of Tuam that the bishops had the game in their hands, and would get all they wished if they only stood firm.* The result proved to be very different; the Bill was read a third time without serious modification, and two generations of young Irishmen fighting the battle of life without adequate discipline, have paid the penalty of mistakes on both sides which rendered futile a beneficent design.

* *Private Correspondence of O'Connell.* (John Murray, 1888.)

In view of O'Connell's return to Dublin, the project of breaking with the friends of mixed education was eagerly debated among the partisans of the " Young Liberator."

Davis wrote to O'Brien :—

"O'Loghlen [Sir Colman] and all whom I have consulted are firm against secession. O'Loghlen proposes, and I agree with him fully, that if O'Connell on his return should force the question on Conciliation Hall, an amendment should be moved that the introduction of such a question, against the wish of a numerous and respectable portion of the committee, is contrary to the principles of the Association and likely to injure the cause of Repeal. A steady elaborate discussion for a number of days would end in the withdrawal of the motion and amendment, or in rendering the motion, if carried, powerless. An explanation would follow, and —the cause would still be safe."

To this opinion O'Brien cordially adhered ; he was not prepared to sacrifice the greater cause to the lesser :—

"I feel entirely the importance to the cause of Repeal of my maintaining sincere, unreserved, and friendly co-operation with O'Connell; but I am bound also to add that, under the present circumstances of our relative positions, I would prefer to withdraw for a time from active efforts in the Association, rather than appear there as an adversary to his policy."*

* O'Brien to Davis, Limerick, December 1, 1844.

Davis replied :—

"I will not interfere again till an attempt be made to pledge the Association to evil resolutions. If the O'Connells wish, they can ruin the agitation (not the country) in spite of anyone. Between unaccounted-for funds, bigotry, billingsgate, Tom Steele missions, crude and contradictory dogmas, and unrelieved stupidity, any cause and any system could be ruined. America, too, from whence arose 'the cloud in the west' which alarmed Peel, has been deeply offended, and but for the NATION there would not now be one Repeal club in America. Still we have a sincere and numerous people, a rising literature, an increasing staff of young, honest, trained men. Peel's splitting policy [a policy which split up the Tories], the chance of war, the chance of the Orangemen, and a great, though now misused, organization; and perhaps next autumn a rally may be made. It will require forethought, close union, indifference to personal attack, and firm measures. At this moment the attempt would utterly fail; but parties may be brought down to reason by the next four months. Again, I tell you, you have no notion of the loss sustained by John O'Connell's course. A dogged temper and a point of honour induce me to remain in the Association at every sacrifice, and will keep me there while there is a chance, even a remote one, of doing good in it."

Here surely was a contest in which men of liberal instincts outside Ireland could scarcely hesitate in choosing sides. But so perverse and intractable are national prejudices that our most bitter assailants were some of the leaders of liberal opinion in England. In an article written by Thackeray, which took the form of a letter from "Mr. Punch (of *Punch*) to Mr. Davis (of the *Nation*)," Davis was turned into contemptuous ridicule for presuming to maintain his opinions against O'Connell, and assured that, since Marat, a more disgusting demagogue had not appeared than himself!

Davis's friends were determined that he should no longer shelter himself from the public recognition of his services. Invitations came to him from the provinces to various public entertainments; but he did not accept any. He was urged to resume the practise of his profession that he might have a neutral field wherein to show what sort of a man he was, and various other projects were mooted in private correspondence. His enemies were equally active; at that time and down to the day of his death he was habitually slandered in private gossip by a herd of blockheads who thought abuse of him a sure road to favour with Mr. John O'Connell, who now posed as victor in the late contest.

When the autumn approached, the leaders of the Association scattered for their usual holiday, and this feeble, barren young man was placed by his father in supreme control of the great popular organization. It is still a point in controversy whether the disastrous use he made of this opportunity was the result of simple incapacity, or of that malicious spirit which the Americans designate " cussedness." It is certain that he wished to rehearse the part of dictator, and was not indisposed to do whatever the Young Irelanders wished to be left undone. Week after week new outrages were committed against the fundamental principles on which the national confederacy rested. It was open to Irishmen of all political opinions who desired the repeal of the Union ; but it was suddenly pledged to a Whig-Radical programme of measures to be obtained at Westminster. It was bound to cultivate the goodwill of friendly nations ; but the two most friendly nations in the world, the only two which took any genuine interest in our affairs, were wantonly insulted. O'Connell himself declared that he would not accept Repeal if it were to be obtained with the assistance of such a people as the French, and on another occasion he proffered England Irish assistance in a conflict with the United States, to pluck down the stripes and stars ! That the Association should be free from sectarian controversy was a condition of its existence ; but week after week harangues were delivered on the German Catholic Church, and the holy coat of Treves. One of the most respectable men in the movement, an adherent of O'Connell from the Clare election down to that day, was asked by the Young Liberator " how he dared " to come to the

Association to remonstrate against the attacks on America as unwise and unnecessary. The evil wrought only concerns us here from the necessity of explaining allusions in Davis's correspondence, which might otherwise be unintelligible.

The move towards Whig-Radicalism greatly alarmed Smith O'Brien, who counted on Tory adhesions. He wrote to Davis :—

"Having received lately intimations of support of the Repeal cause from quarters in which I did not in the least expect to find it, I am doubly disappointed in finding that the policy about to be adopted by the leaders of the Association is such as to destroy all my hopes of immediate progress."*

Of the attack on America, Dillon wrote to Davis :—

"Everybody is indignant at O'Connell meddling in the business. His talk about bringing down the pride of the American Eagle, if England would pay us sufficiently, is not merely foolish, but false and base. Such talk must be supremely disgusting to the Americans, and to every man of honour and spirit."

The effect of the mispolicy was speedy and signal in America. The Repeal Associations in Baltimore, New Orleans, and other cities were dissolved, and the

* July 23, 1845.

native press was furious against Irish ingratitude. But the attack on individual liberty outraged Dillon more than the blunders in public policy.

"I have just read," he wrote to Davis, "with inexpressible disgust, the speech of John O'Connell, and the scene which followed between himself and Scott. It behoves you to consider very seriously whether the NATION is not bound to notice this matter. . . . My notion is that Scott has a right to protection, and that the public will, or ought to, feel indignant if this protection be withheld. The NATION could not possibly get a better opportunity of reading a long required lecture to Johnny. The immediate topic is one on which public opinion is universally against him. . . . [Mr. Scott, who was an old man long associated with O'Connell, and having no relation with the Young Irelanders, made a slight effort to pacify America by excluding from Conciliation Hall Negro slavery, Texas, Oregon, and the whole range of Transatlantic questions upon which O'Connell and Mr. John O'Connell had been haranguing.] Can anything be more evident than the puerile folly of it? When the Americans were engaged in their own struggle only fancy one of their orators coming down to the Congress with a violent invective against the abuses of the French Government of the day. Any man who is thoroughly in earnest about one thing cannot allow his mind to wander in pursuit of things not merely unconnected, but inconsistent with that thing. It is impossible latterly to bear with the insolence of this little frog. There is no man or country safe from his venom. If there be not some protest against him, he will set the whole world against us."

Somewhat later he wrote, " In this county [Mayo], as far as I can see, Repeal is all but extinct."

But the public blunders of the maladroit tribune did not exhaust his energies ; he found time to stimulate the calumnies on Davis and his friends. From Tipperary, Doheny wrote to Davis :—

"It [the NATION] is in great disrepute among the priests. I met a doctor at Nenagh who lost two subscribers to a dispensary for refusing to give it up, . . . I was thinking of writing an article on the subject. If you and Duffy don't approve of it when you see it, it can be left out. O'Connell's HINTS are taken to be corroborative of the ruffianism of others."

MacNevin's impetuous nature could not silently wait events. He wrote to me at this time :—

"Dillon is sick of the abomination of desolation on Burgh quay. It never opens its sooty mouth on the subject of Repeal now. By the way, where is the Repeal Agitation? Is it hunting at Derrynane? . . . My Parliamentary mania is cured; I would not accept the representation of any constituency at the beck of such a body. I will work with you and Davis, but no more with the base melange of tyranny and mendicancy. I am glad that Davis does not go to the Association; I shall not go when I return."

The most respectable of the recent recruits began to waver. Grey Porter had retired, and Hely Hutchinson declined to enter Parliament, though a southern

Q

county was offered to him. This was the condition of public affairs a few weeks after the question of the provincial colleges was forced upon the Repeal Association.

I have not tacked to any transaction in this narrative the moral which it suggests ; the thoughtful reader prefers to draw his own conclusions. But for once I ask Irish Protestants to note the conduct of Catholic young men in a mortal contest. The veteran leader of the people, sure to be backed by the whole force of the unreflecting masses, and supported on this occasion by the bulk of the national clergy—a man of genius, an historic man wielding an authority made august by a life's services, discredited Thomas Davis, and was able, few men doubted, to overwhelm him and his sympathisers in political ruin. A public career might be closed for all of us ; our journal might be extinguished ; we were already denounced as intriguers and infidels ; it was quite certain that by-and-by, we would be described as hirelings of the Castle. But Davis was right ; and of all his associates, not one man flinched from his side,—not one man. A crisis bringing character to a sharper test has never arisen in our history, nor can ever arise ; and the conduct of these men, it seems to me, is some guarantee how their successors would act in any similar emergency.

CHAPTER VIII.

A NEW DEPARTURE. 1845.

NDER these checks and discouragements Davis did not fall back, but pressed forward. When the sky was clear he would gladly have retired for a time, but when the wind was high, and the horizon dark, retirement was impossible. To attend Conciliation Hall was indeed a waste of life, but the special work of the *Nation*, "mind-making," as he named it, remained, and he threw himself into it with admirable industry. It is necessary for parties to cast the lead from time to time, and "take an observation" in order to know their actual progress ; and the late controversy enabled us to measure the gain in self-reliance and independent opinion which the middle-class had attained, and taught us to set our hopes on a sure but distant future. It is pathetic, almost tragic, to note the use Davis made of what proved to be the last months of his life.

Only the work of a Minister of State, controlling a great department, can equal the variety of interests on which he had to issue instructions, tender advice, or call for information. He sat in his little book-lined den in Bagot Street, or in his bureau at the *Nation* office, and moved a hundred minds to furnish the data on which conclusions are founded, or to carry out suggestions for promoting our main design.

I found among his papers a list of agenda, probably prepared about this time. Some of the work has been since done, but whatever remains incomplete has a valid claim upon the young men of to-day :—

1. Maps of Ireland (historical, and for practical use) A large map ; and little guide-book plans with sketches of every ruin.

2. Historical Buildings, Pictures, Busts, Statues, etc., in our Towns.

3. Irish Almanacs (Irish letter-paper, with music, landscapes, emblems, historical designs, etc.)

4. A Musical Circulating Library (established by a club, and allowing counties to subscribe).

5. Irish Biographical Dictionary.

6. Absentee List [a roll of the owners of Irish estates who were non-resident].

7. History of the War from 1641 to 1652.

8. Military History of 1798.

9. Former Commerce with Denmark and Spain.

10. Irish Statistics (each county separately, as in Scotland).

11. An Illustrated History.

12. Restoration of Churches, etc.

13. Reprint of Historical Pamphlets.

14. Lives of Illustrious Irishmen—Brian Boru, Dathi, Nial, Columba, Columbkille, Malachi, Duns Scotus, St. Lawrence, Cathal, Donald O'Brien, McCarthy (with family notes and antiquarian authorities), Lodge, Cambrensis, Lynch, O'Donovan's Annals of the Four Masters, Hallam, Keating, O'Halloran, O'Flaherty, Byrne, Art O'Kavanagh (see Irish Annals), Kildare, Shane O'Neil, Hugh O'Donnell, Tirone, Settlement of Ulster, Roger O'More, Owen Roe and his brothers, etc., Ormond, Tirconnell, Sarsfield, Molyneux, Swift, Lucas, Flood, Grattan, Tone.

The once simple programme of the National party had become a tangled skein, but he pushed controversy aside, and applied all his strength to the purpose of training the people for freer lives and higher duties hereafter.

Maddyn, whom he desired to draw more and more into this work, pleaded that he had undertaken duties in connection with *Hood's Magazine*, and that he, too, was in search of recruits :—

"Hood's lamented illness has kept them back, but it will go on, and no mistake, for Spottiswoode, the great printer, is the capitalist of the magazine. It will, I think, merge into a Liberal organ before long, as the editor of it is biassed that way. Have you anything that you would give them? Turn it over in your mind. The magazine sells three thousand a month, and your writings would certainly be seen,

Do you think Duffy could be got to give some of his poems for it—even one short paper would be of value?"

At this time I submitted to my comrades a project which next to the establishment of the *Nation*, produced the most permanent results. The project was to publish a monthly volume of history, poetry, or fiction, calculated to feed the national spirit or discipline the national morals; and millions of these books have since been printed and are in the hands of Irishmen all over the world. It is not at all wonderful that writers ignorant of the facts have attributed the design to Davis, so fertile in design, but it was wholly mine. He took it up with enthusiasm, but he died before the third volume was published, and I had not his invaluable aid in carrying it out. Early in the autumn Davis wrote to Pigot that the project was launched :—

"Our Library of Ireland promises better than any other undertaking of our party, and, what is better still, is likely to be aided by Whigs and Tories.

"The American hurrah for us, and against O'C.'s speech [on Federalism], was a useful diversion.

". . . Johnny has thrown the agitation two years back. John Dillon doing well. C. G. D. better than ever in his life. Myself in good health of body and in a CALM mood—after a storm; you know the proverb."

Shortly after, he wrote to the same correspondent :—

"August 5th, 1845.

"C. G. D.'s ballad volume is at its third edition, really BONA FIDE, and will, I am sure, sell 10,000 copies.

"He and every one gone to the country, and I am alone, anxious for various reasons; but in work, and that is a shield from most assaults on the mind."

The success of the library was an infinite pleasure to Davis, and he reported it exultingly to his friends. To O'Brien he wrote :—

"What of Sarsfield's statue? I think Moore would like to do it [Christopher Moore, who had made effective busts of Curran and Plunket, but proved on trial to be unequal to statues]. Kirk is not competent. The 'Ballad Poetry' has reached a third edition, and cannot be printed fast enough for the sale. It is every way good. Not an Irish Conservative of education but will read it, and be brought nearer to Ireland by it. That is a propagandism worth a thousand harangues such as you ask me to make."

O'Brien replied :—

"I cannot but hope that the publication of the monthly volume will be of infinite value to the national cause, if the intellectual and moral standard of the work can be kept as high as it ought to be. I like the two first numbers very much—I could not lay down the 'Ballads' until I had read the whole volume. I am delighted with the article in yesterday's NATION respecting the prospect of a union between Orange and Green. It makes me for a moment believe that the dream of my life is about to be realized. I know that I could not recommend [in the Association] that a few hundred copies of this number of the NATION should be sent into the Orange districts, without awakening jealousies which it is very unadvisable to raise ; but I think it worth while the consideration of you and Duffy, whether it would not be well to print this article on separate slips of paper, and send them by post into the heart of Fermanagh."

To a similar announcement Maddyn replied :

"The 'Ballad Poetry of Ireland' is admirable. It is all to nothing the best edited collection I ever saw. The introduction is a choice specimen of writing ; it merits what the SPECTATOR said of it—and what more could be desired ? It reflects immense credit on Duffy."

The early death of John Banim, the national novelist, who shared the political hopes of his race, left his widow ill provided. As the Executive had the disposal of an annual grant for literary pensions derived in part from Irish taxes, it was resolved to claim a provision for her from that source. A committee was organized by the writers of the *Nation*, and it was considered at the time a note of progress that the men who composed it should have consented to act together for any purpose. They were :—Daniel O'Connell, M.P., John Anster, LL.D. (the translator of *Faust*), Smith O'Brien, M.P., Isaac Butt, LL.D. (then leader of the extreme Conservatives), Dr. Kane (since Sir Robert Kane), John O'Connell, M.P.,

Charles Lever (the author of *Harry Lorrequer*), Torrens McCullagh, LL.B (since McCullagh Torrens), Thomas Davis, Samuel Ferguson (the late Sir Samuel Ferguson, Deputy Keeper of the Records in Ireland), Thomas O'Hagan (since Lord O'Hagan), William Carleton (author of *Traits and Stories of the Irish Peasantry*), E. B. Roche, M.P. (since Lord Fermoy), Joseph Le Fanu (author of *The House by the Churchyard*, etc.), Charles Gavan Duffy, Hubert Smith, M.R.I.A., Thomas MacNevin, Dr. Maunsell (editor of the *Evening Mail*), Grey Porter (still assiduous in Irish affairs half a century later), James M'Glashan (proprietor of the *Dublin University Magazine*), and M. J. Barry.

The committee succeeded, through the agency of A. B. Roche mainly, in inducing Sir Robert Peel to grant a small pension to Mrs. Banim.*

---

* The surviving author of the *Tales of the O'Hara Family*, who, in politics, was an unswerving adherent of O'Connell, acknowledged that this service to his brother's widow was attributable to the new men.

"DEAR SIR,—I beg to return you my very sincere thanks for the very effectual performance of your promise to me, in my sister-in-law's business. However others may have worked in the matter, I impute it solely to your kindness that such success has been the result; and I will always regard you as the person to whom my brother's widow is really indebted.

"I am, dear sir, your obliged servant,

"M. BANIM.

"Kilkenny, May 10, 1845.
"Chas. Gavan Duffy, Esq."

As the autumn approached, Davis wrote to Maddyn that he was disturbed by a serious personal trouble. The trouble was one rarely wanting as a motor in the lives of young men; he was in love. When he began to write verse, one of his friends who thought a Laura was an essential part of the equipment of a Petrarch, asked him if he had ever been in love. " I have never been out of it," was his laughing reply. But these amourettes were passing fancies, and his profound nature craved a great and permanent passion. At length he encountered the girl who was to rule his life. Annie Hutton was the only daughter of Thomas Hutton, whom we had already heard of as a leading Federalist—an opulent and honourable citizen who had sat in the House of Commons for a time as member for Dublin, and still took a lively interest in public affairs. When Davis met her she was barely twenty years of age, a slender, graceful girl with features of classic contour and marble hue. He has painted her in graphic verse :—

> " Her eyes are darker than Dunloe,
> Her soul is whiter than the snow,
> Her tresses like arbutus flow,
>   Her step like frighted deer :
> Then, still thy waves, capricious lake !
> And ceaseless, soft winds, round her wake.
> Yet never bring a cloud to break
>   The smile of Annie dear ! "

The proverbial impediments which bar the course of true love did not spring in this case from the coldness of the lady. His songs are those of a happy lover. But at thirty years of age, when the responsibilities of manhood awaited him, it was too plain that he had sacrificed professional advancement, and all that is vulgarly called success, to public duty. He was a perfect publicist, but in Ireland the national journalist carried on his work under the constant risk of ruinous State prosecution. And while his acquaintance with Miss Hutton was still young there broke out, on the other hand, as we have seen, a storm of bigotry which threatened to drive him from public life. If a prudent father consented to overlook the insecurity of his worldly position, a generous lover could not shut his own eyes to it.

It is pleasant to know that no impediment finally separated the noblest heart beating in Ireland at that hour from the woman he loved. During the most stringent labours of the period just past in review, he became the affianced lover of Miss Hutton. A single note from the lady will sufficiently indicate the frank and chivalrous relations established between them. The love of Davis raises his promised bride far above the region of conventionality, and makes whatever concerns her of an interest like that which kindles for the Beatrice of Dante, the sympathy and solicitude of a nation.

"How shall I tell you how happy I was to get your dear, dear letter, for which I love you twenty times better than before, for now you are treating me with confidence, not like a child whom it pleases you to play with. Do you know that was (but it is nearly gone) the one fear I had, that you would think of me as a plaything, more than as a friend; but I don't think you will since last night. There now, dearest, you have all that is on my mind. . . . Oh! I forgot I intended to begin this with a profound scolding; I am really very angry with you for writing my unworthy name in that beautiful book of 'Melodies.' Indeed, you must not, dearest, be giving me so many books; besides, I like better to have them when they are yours."

Miss Hutton's mother, who was a woman of notable capacity and accomplishments, one of the gifted circle whom Miss Mitford called her friends, valued and esteemed Davis, understood the nobility of his character and the vigour of his intellect, but was far from being in sympathy with the main purpose of his life. This was a trouble he had long encountered in his own family, among those whom he loved best, and who loved him best; and here again it became evident that difference of conviction would not prevent the lady from being a gracious and considerate *belle-mère*.

During these crowded months, the period of his hardest work and most exulting happiness, he ripened notably in health, spirits, and self-confidence. "All who remember him during that time," says one of his friends, "can testify to the wonderful change he underwent even in appearance. His form dilated, his eyes got a new fire, his step was firmer, and the look of a proud purpose sat on him." *

* Mr. Justice O'Hagan.

CHAPTER IX.

DEATH OF THOMAS DAVIS. 1845.

N the midst of this generous and fruitful work,—on the threshold, as it seemed, of a long and happy career,—when his power to stimulate and control his generation was greatest and most stringently needed,—from the midst of a crowd of loyal friends, and from the side of the woman he had wooed and won for his bride, Thomas Davis, by God's inscrutable judgment, received the summons which none can resist—the strong no more than the weak. On the 9th of September, 1845, he did not appear at the *Nation* office as usual, but a note came from him announcing what he believed to be a slight stomachic derangement :—

"Tuesday morning.

"MY DEAR D.—I have had an attack of some sort of cholera, and PERHAPS have slight scarlatina. I cannot see any one, and am in bed. Don't be alarmed about me; but don't rely on my being able to write.

"Ever yours,—T. D."

The lines were somewhat tremulous, but as I learned from his servant that the note was written in bed, the change from his usual clear and vigorous handwriting excited no suspicion. The brave young man, tossing in feverish pain, was thinking chiefly of duties necessarily neglected for a time, and of the risk that news of his condition in some alarming shape should reach the heart which it would wound the sorest. After a couple of days he wrote to me again :—

"DEAR D.—I have had a bad attack of scarlatina, with a horrid sore throat; don't mention this to ANY one for a very delicate reason I have; but pray get the Curran's speeches read, except the Newry election. Have Conway's POST of 1812 sent back to him, and read and correct yourself so much of the memoir as I sent In four days I hope to be able to look at light business for a short time.—Ever yours—T. D."

The handwriting in this note was still more blurred and tremulous than in the first, but the tone was so confident, and the reliance of his comrades on the vigour of his constitution, which seemed safe against all the mischances of life, was so complete, that they banished all apprehension. His mother and sister, whom he tenderly loved, and who loved him with passionate affection, were at his bedside. Dr. Stokes, a physician in the first rank of his profession, was in attendance ; and no one doubted that in a week or so he would be at his post again. I replied to his second note as one does to a friend absent for a day or two, by some casual mischance :—

"MY DEAR DAVIS—I will do all you desire forthwith. When may I hope to see you? Leave word with your servant when you are well enough to be seen. I cannot now keep your illness a secret, because I told John O'Hagan and M'Carthy yesterday ; but I will prevent them going to see you. John says you have an opportunity of rivalling Mirabeau, by dying at this minute ; but he begs you won't be tempted by the inviting opportunity.—Always yours—C. G. D."

Towards the end of the week he improved greatly ; so greatly that he insisted on driving out for an hour for a purpose which may be conjectured with considerable confidence. A relapse followed this imprudence, but not a whisper of danger was heard. On Tuesday morning, September 15th, I was summoned to his mother's house to see his dead body. Never in a long life has a stroke so wholly unexpected fallen on me. There lay the man whom I loved beyond any on the earth, a pallid corpse. His face still wore the character of sweet silent strength which marked it when he lived, and it was hard to believe that I should never more feel his cordial clasping hand, or see his eyes beaming with affection and sincerity. He had grown rapidly worse during the night time, but was confident of recovery until almost the end, and spoke impatiently of interrupted work. At dawn he died in the arms of Neville, a faithful servant, who had been in constant attendance on him.

I immediately communicated the tragic news to his closest friends who were absent from Dublin. It was received with wails of pain and dismay.* Not one

* "Your letter," Dillon wrote me, "was like a thrust from a dagger. I had not even heard that he was unwell. This calamity makes the world look black. God knows I am tempted to wish myself well out of it. I am doing you a grievous wrong to leave you alone at this melancholy time. I was preparing to be off by the post-car, but my friends have one and all protested against it, and I verily believe that they would keep me by force if nothing else would. God help us, my dear fellow; I don't know how we can look at one another when we meet."

"I have been," wrote MacNevin, "in a state of the greatest agony since I got your letter last evening. I could have lost nearer than he with less anguish;—he was such a noble, gentle creature. And to me always exaggerating my good qualities, never finding fault, and never, never with an angry look or word. He was more than a brother; and I loved him better than all the brothers I have. Our bond of union is broken; what mournful meetings ours will be in future. . . . My God, how horror-struck will be Dillon and Smith O'Brien! I never closed my eyes since I got the fatal news."

A few days later he wrote: "I feel so lonely and bereaved, the soul has gone out of all my hopes for the future, and even

R

of them, it may be confidently surmised, had conceived the possibility that the strong man might disappear without a moment's notice, and carry with him
much that was most precious in their lives. I have
already written what I saw and felt on that occasion,

the conviction of the dear friends I have still goes but a short
way to reconcile me to a loss that I know is irreparable. I had
a mournful satisfaction in reading the beautiful tribute in the
Nation to his extraordinary virtues."

Maddyn wrote in a more subdued tone of affection, which
men of his opinions, for he was a Unionist, may still read with
profit : —

"I need not say how your letter stunned me. I can hardly
credit the intelligence still. With no one in this world did I
more sympathise. I never loved any man so much, and I respected him just as much. The man Thomas Davis ought to be
exhibited in as strong colours as consist with truth, not only to
his countrymen but to the citizens of this empire. The world
must be told what his nature was, how large and patriotic were
his designs, and how truly pure were his purposes. For he was
one of those spirits who quicken others by communication with
them. For the purpose of recording his career in a literary
shape, I venture to suggest that his personal friends should
meet and determine that his life should be given to the public,
and that all of them should contribute whatever materials they
could to such a work. You ought to be the recorder of his life ;
for that office you of all his friends are the most fitted, not alone by
talents and literary power, but by thoroughly close and catholic
sympathy with the noble Davis in all things. There was more
of the *idem velle* and *idem nolle* between him and you than between any other of that large circle who admired him living and
lament him dead. Your close intimacy and identification for
the last three memorable years, your agreement with him on all
practical and speculative questions of Irish politics, your personal
cognizance of the extent of his unseen labours to serve the
country he loved—these things seem to command that you
honour yourself and your friend by taking charge of his memory.
Let me entreat of you to resolve upon doing so."

and I prefer borrowing the narrative to telling the same tale in other words.

"Though it was the season when Dublin was emptiest of the cultivated class, a public funeral was immediately determined upon by a few leading men, and the assent of his family obtained. But it was no cold funereal pageantry that accompanied him to the grave. In all the years of my life, before and since, I have not seen so many grown men weep bitter tears as on that September day. The members of the 'Eighty-two Club, the Corporation of Dublin, and the Committee of the Repeal Association took their place in the procession as a matter of course; but it would have soothed the spirit of Davis to see mixed with the green uniforms and scarlet gowns, men of culture and intellect without distinction of party and outside of all political parties. The antiquaries and scholars of the Royal Irish Academy, the Councils of the Archæological and Celtic Societies, the artists of the Royal Hibernian Academy, the committee of the Dublin Library, sent deputations, and the names best known in Irish literature and art might be read next day in the long list of mourners. He was buried in Mount Jerome Cemetery, in latter years the burying-place of the Protestant community, but once the pleasure-grounds of the suburban villa where John Keogh, the Catholic leader, took counsel with Wolfe Tone, the young Protestant patriot, how to unite the jarring creeds in a common struggle for Ireland. The Whig and Conservative Press did him generous justice. They recognized in him a man unbiassed by personal ambition and untainted by the rancour of faction, who loved but never flattered his countrymen; and who, still in the very prime of manhood, was regarded not only with

affection and confidence, but with veneration, by his
associates. The first proposal for a monument came
from a Tory; and Whigs and Tories rivalled his political friends in carrying the project to completion.
To the next meeting of the Association, O'Connell
wrote : 'I solemnly declare that I never knew any man
who could be so useful to Ireland in the present stage
of the struggle.' O'Brien on the same occasion described him as one who 'united a woman's tenderness
with the soul of a hero.' Even Mr. John O'Connell
discovered, somewhat late in the day, that 'if there
did exist differences of opinion (between Davis and
other Nationalists) they were differences of honest and
sincere conviction.' But the bulk of the people
throughout the island little knew the calamity that had
befallen them. A writer of the period compared them
to children who had lost their father, and were unconscious of all the danger and trouble such a fact
implied.

"Judging him now, a generation after his death,
when years and communion with the world have
tempered the exaggerations of youthful friendship,
I can confidently affirm that I have not known a man
so nobly gifted as Thomas Davis. If his articles had
been spoken speeches his reputation as an orator would
have rivalled Grattan's, and the beauty and vigour of
his style were never employed for mere show, as they
sometimes were by Grattan; he fired not rockets, but
salvos of artillery. If his programmes and reports, which
were the plans and specifications of much of the best
work done in his day, had been habitually associated
with his name, his practical genius would have ranked
as high as O'Connell's. Among his comrades who were
poets he would have been chosen Laureate, though
poetry was only his pastime. And these gifts leave

his rarest qualities untold. What he was as a friend, so tender, so helpful, so steadfast, no description will paint. His comrades had the same careless confidence in him men have in the operations of nature, where irregularity and aberration do not exist. Like Burke and Berkeley, he inspired and controlled all who came within the range of his influence, without aiming to lead or dominate. He was singularly modest and unselfish. In a long life I have never known any man remotely resemble him in these qualities. The chief motive-power of a party and a cause, labouring for them as a man of exemplary industry labours in his calling, he not only never claimed any recognition or reward, but discouraged allusion to his services by those who knew them best.

. Passionate enthusiasm is apt to become prejudice, but in Davis it was controlled not only by a disciplined judgment but by a fixed determination to be just. He brought to political controversy a fairness previously unexampled in Ireland. In all his writings there will not be found a single sentence reflecting ungenerously on any human being. He had set himself the task of building up a nation, a task not beyond his strength had fortune been kind. Now that the transactions of that day have fallen into their natural perspective, now that we know what has perished and what survives of its conflicting opinions, we may plainly see, that, imperfectly as they knew him, the Irish race—the grown men of 1845—in the highest diapason of their passions, in the widest range of their capacity for action or endurance, were represented and embodied in Thomas Davis better than in any man then living. He had predicted a revolution; and if fundamental change in the ideas which move and control a people be a revolution, then his prediction was already accomplished. In conflicts of opinion near at hand a prodigious change made itself manifest, traceable to teaching of which he was the chief exponent. During his brief career, scarcely exceeding three years, he had administered no office of authority, mounted no tribune, published no books, or next to none, and marshalled no following; but with the simplest agencies, in the columns of a newspaper, in casual communication with his friends and contemporaries, he made a name which, after a generation, is still recalled with enthusiasm or tears, and will be dear to students and patriots while there is an Irish people."*

From the death-bed of my friend, I passed at a stride to the death-bed of my young wife, and was for a moment unfit for work. But my absence proved a gain. The article in the *Nation* announcing Davis's death and burial, which attracted much attention at the time, was written by one who did not share his opinions or mine, but who honoured Davis's great gifts, and was never more at home than when coming to the aid of a friend in a critical emergency. The late Lord O'Hagan, then a young barrister, every moment of whose time was bespoken for professional business, did me this essential service.

Davis's friends determined to make him known to the world for what he truly was. A committee of leading men of the metropolis, without distinction of party,

* *Young Ireland,* book iii., chap. x.

commissioned John Hogan to carve his statue in white marble. Mr. Burton,* who knew and loved him, without sharing his political opinions, painted his portrait. I wrote a brief memoir of him in the *Nation*. A selection was made from his historical and antiquarian essays, and his poems were collected and carefully edited.† Elegies were written on his memory by his most distinguished contemporaries. A verse from Ferguson's elegy will adequately represent them all:—

"I walked through Ballinderry in the springtime,
    When the bud was on the tree;
And I said, in every fresh-ploughed field beholding
    The sowers striding free,
Scattering broadcast forth the corn in golden plenty,
    On the quick seed-clasping soil,
Even such, this day, among the fresh-stirred hearts of
    Erin,
    Thomas Davis, is thy toil."

---

* The present Sir Frederic Burton.

† The poems were edited by Thomas Wallis, the essays by Gavan Duffy. Shortly after his death Ferguson estimated his labours in the *Dublin University Magazine*, the mouthpiece of the Conservative majority, more generously than would have been possible while he was still an active combatant in current politics. "They (the Young Irelanders) sought," he says, "to teach the people justice, manliness, and reliance on themselves; to supplant vanity on the one hand, and servility on the other, by a just self-appreciation and proper pride; to make them sensible that nothing could be had without labour, and nothing enjoyed without prudence; to teach them to scorn the baseness of foul play, and that if they were to fight, they should fight like men and soldiers—these were the lessons which he now appeared a chosen instrument for imparting; and in fulfilling this mission, while Providence left him with us, he did toil with faithful and unremitting energy."

It is the sure fate of a feeble fire to go out and be forgotten; but Davis's reputation has gone on gathering increased light and heat for nearly half a century. Men and women who were not born when he was amongst us, rival his personal friends in devotion. A young Celtic poetess who only became acquainted with his writings after his death, exclaimed, "Might not one such Protestant make us forget the Penal Laws?" A young Protestant patriot of Saxon pedigree, who shares many of Davis's gifts as well as his opinions, made a new and more exhaustive collection of his essays for English readers fifty years after the Dublin edition. Welsh publicists and politicians are proud to claim him as a scion of their race, whose aims they applaud and whose character they honour. Moore left behind him youthful erotics, for which in his old age he not only blushed but wept. It needs a large charity towards the sins of genius to pardon the loose life and vagrant muse of Burns. The noble, personal independence of Béranger, who would not accept fee or favour from any party, who refused to be presented to the Citizen King, to sit in the Republican Assembly, or to touch the gifts of the Bonapartes, cannot make us forget that his *chansons graveleuses* have, perhaps, corrupted the morals of France as decisively as his patriotic songs fortified its public spirit. But there is not one impure thought in the poetry or prose of Davis.

The grevious blow which so suddenly destroyed Miss Hutton's happiness shortened her life. "She faded away," says a friend who knew her well, "from the hour of his death." One task alone interested her : he had asked her to translate from the Italian, *The Embassy in Ireland of Monsignor Rinuccini,* which lights up a period of profound historical interest. But the task was beyond her strength, and the book was only completed and published by her mother twenty years after her death. She died on the 7th of June, 1853, in the twenty-eighth year of her age, and will live long in the memory of those who love and honour Thomas Davis.

In one of her latest letters she raises a question which none of us can evade—the question : What would have befallen if Davis had not died? Our history is full of problems like this. If Swift had accepted the Captain's commission which William III. offered him ? If Phelim O'Neill had been captured with Lord Maguire ? If Tone had been permitted to colonize his island in the Pacific ? If Hoche had landed in Munster ? If a mitigation of the penal laws had not opened the Bar to O'Connell, but left him a discontented squireen in Munster ? Any one of these casual circumstances might have turned backward the current of our history. If Davis had not died, he would probably have been driven out of the Repeal Association, with Smith O'Brien, when the new Whig compact was completed in 1847, and he would have brought to Tipperary in '48 the foresight, will, and resources of a born soldier.   He would not have succeeded, for the time for success was past, but he would have failed gloriously.   As it is, has he not succeeded gloriously?   His spirit has palpably animated whatever generous work was undertaken for Ireland from the day of his death to this hour.   His comrades, while they survived, carried the opinions which they shared with him into literature and public life, into confederacies and parliaments, into prison and exile, and never failed to take up the Irish question again and again while life remained.   A new generation, scattered over three continents, has found inspiration in his writings, even when they have sometimes wandered aside from the broad and noble highway which he traced out for Irish liberty.   It is easy now to see that the work for which he was fittest was to be a teacher, and he is still one of the most persuasive and beloved teachers of his race; but beyond the pregnant thoughts he uttered, and the noble strains he sang, the life he led was the greatest lesson he has bequeathed to them.

THE STORY OF
EARLY GAELIC LITERATURE.

BY

DOUGLAS HYDE, LL.D.

NEW LIBRARY OF IRELAND, Vol. VI.

NOTICES OF THE PRESS.

"The story of 'Early Gaelic Literature' is the title of the latest work added to the rapidly growing series of the New Irish Library. The author is Dr. Douglas Hyde, and the book, though issued in an unpretentious form by Mr. T. Fisher Unwin is of the rarest interest to every student of Irish literature. . . . Books like that of Dr. Hyde are lights in the van of advancement."—IRISH TIMES, March 8th, 1895. Leading article on the book.

"Dr. Hyde has the ideal scholarly qualities, the patience, the enthusiasm, the research, the love of his work, and he has in addition the power of placing before us the knowledge he has collected with a literary skill and charm that lift his work out of the category of the specialist. . . . We hope this addition to the New Irish Library will sell by tens of thousands in Ireland. It is informed with more knowledge, sympathy, and power of imparting knowledge that many rich tomes on the shelves of wealthy collectors and in college libraries. A rich shilling's-worth! It makes us thirsty for more yet to come from this fountain-head."—DAILY INDEPENDENT. Leading article on the book, March 15th, 1895.

"One could not have a pleasanter or a more accomplished guide to the beauties of the treasure-house of Irish poetry and romance. His translations, while preserving as much as possible of the colour, style, and even accent of the original, are excellently done, and are in themselves good literature."—FREEMAN'S JOURNAL, March 17th, 1895.

"Those who read the Story of Early Gaelic Literature should not omit to read its preface, for it is one of the most remarkable parts of a remarkable book. . . . The Story of Early Gaelic Literature is a book of which every Irishman, no matter what his creed may be, should feel proud. It is a noble work on a noble theme, and it is to be hoped its gifted author will produce many more like it."—DAILY EXPRESS, March 21st, 1895.

"To the true Celtic Irishman it will be as wine to warm his blood, one of the noblest vindications ever penned of the learning, the genius, and the civilization of the far-scattered, but indestructable race of the Clanna-Gael."—UNITED IRELAND, March 30th, 1895.

"In the Story of Early Gaelic Literature is given to the public a book which we trust no Irishman pretending to interest in national matters will neglect to read. . . . Dr. Hyde set before himself what to him is a pleasant task, and he has fulfilled it in a manner beyond all praise."—EVENING TELEGRAPH, March 9th, 1895.

Preparing for Immediate Publication

A FINAL EDITION

OF

YOUNG IRELAND.

A FRAGMENT OF IRISH HISTORY 1842-1846.

Illustrated with Portraits, Autographs, Facsimilies and Historical Scenes.

BY THE

HON. SIR C. GAVAN DUFFY, K.C.M.G.

———

To be published in two parts, 2s. each, largely illustrated, and in a volume handsomely bound, price 5s.

———

OPINIONS OF THE CRITICAL PRESS.

From the SATURDAY REVIEW.

" The party which **Davis** created, and of which **Duffy** took the leadership from his hand, had many engaging characteristics, and these characteristics had never been so effectively set out before. The author abstained to a great extent from that curse of Irish controversy—indiscriminate and personal abuse of those who differed with him. The reception of YOUNG IRELAND was thus favourable even with those who could least admit its author's political postulates, or arrive at his historical standpoint. It was recognized as a valuable contribution to history where the author spoke with personal knowledge, and an interesting contribution to literature even where he did not."

From THE TIMES.

"The gifted and ill-fated Party of Young Ireland certainly deserved an APOLOGIA, and it is past dispute that no one could be more competent for the task than Sir Charles Gavan Duffy. Notwithstanding the genuine modesty with which he always attributes the origin of the school (for, in the true sense, it was a school rather than a party) to Thomas Davis, he will, we think, be always regarded as its true founder. He established and guided from 1842 to 1855 the NATION, which was in those days its one accepted organ. A State prisoner with O'Connell in 1844, with Smith O'Brien in 1848, three times tried, and all but convicted of treason in 1848, he organized, after his release from prison, a peaceful agitation for the measures which afterwards formed the main achievements of Mr. Gladstone's Irish policy. Proceeding to Australia in 1855, he has been some time Prime Minister of Victoria and Speaker, and while he filled the chair it is said order reigned in that tumultuous Parliament."

From THE EDINBURGH REVIEW.

"These, it seems, were the founders, heroes, and martyrs of the NATION, and we are free to confess that the Young Ireland of those days had incomparably more patriotism, eloquence, and energy than their degenerate successors. But even Ireland cannot produce an inexhaustible supply of Davises and Duffys. It is in the nature of all human things :—

'In pejus ruere et retro sublapsa referri.' "

From The Dublin Review.

"The remarkable and romantic career of the author serves to stimulate the curiosity of the public; but, independently of those advantages, this book contains literary merit of too high an order, and historical matter of too great value, to allow of its being, under any circumstances, ignored or forgotten. . . , In the vivid description of persons he greatly excels; a few graphic touches and the man stands before us like a picture."

From The Nineteenth Century.

"No doubt the Young Ireland movement contributed greatly, as Sir Charles Duffy contends, to purify and ennoble the national agitation. It substituted for the crafty and often vacillating plans of O'Connell's later years, an open, direct, and generous national policy. As a revolutionary movement it was a failure. It had not got to the heart of the peasantry. The influence it has since had upon the Irish people has sunk gradually with time into their minds and their feelings. In that way it is more powerful to-day than it was in its own time."—JUSTIN McCARTHY, M.P.

From The Contemporary Review.

"I cannot dismiss the volume without bearing witness to his scrupulously fair treatment of those—some of them no longer able to defend themselves—with whom he came into conflict. He is eminently fair to O'Connell, and finds excuses for him even when he is obliged to condemn him."—REV CANON MacCALL.

From The Tablet.

"But the public mind of England, of Europe, of America, and of Australia will listen with interest to the

solemn utterances of such a man as Sir Charles Gavan
Duffy. A strong advocate for constitutional Goverment,
abhorring anarchy, his whole public life, for the last forty
years, is the best pledge of the soundness and sincerity of
his matured opinions. The dream of his young manhood
was to follow in the footsteps of Roger O'More and the
Confederate Catholics of 1641, and identify the faith
with the nationality of Ireland. Associated with Davis,
Dillon, and others, he founded the NATION, October,
1842, and, faithful to his aim of 'Nationality,' he ex-
panded the controversy from merely Catholic to
common Irish interests. His public life in Ireland, in
the Press, in the Repeal movement, in prison, with
O'Connell in 1844, in founding the Irish Confederation;
in the abortive attempt at a rising in 1848; in the
State prosecutions against him that year; in the Tenant
League; and in Parliament from 1852 to 1856, is
familiar to the world. And his colonial career in
Victoria, from his settlement there in 1856, is perhaps
the most brilliant which ever fell to the lot of an
Irish exile."

From THE FREEMAN'S JOURNAL (Dublin).

"APOLOGIA PRO SOCIIS MEIS: So Sir Gavan Duffy
might have fitly named this book. Suppressing himself
so far as it was at all possible in narrating a history
of which he was so great a part, he has devoted un-
wearied labour and a literary power which has few rivals
to the task of raising an enduring memorial to his old
associates, friends, and fellow-workmen; and he has
done this with an enthusiasm and freshness of zealous
conviction which fill every reader of his work with wonder. How vivid it all is! Five-and-twenty years ago
Mr. Duffy left Ireland, struck down, not only by the

catastrophe of 1848, but by a second discomfiture—the failure of his efforts, in company with Frederick Lucas and George Henry Moore, in the cause of the Irish tenant. In the Australian land, to which, in sad discouragement he bent his way, he found the career denied to him at home. Fortune, distinction, eminence awaited him. In that land sons and daughters grew around him. A son of his but the other day held a high position in the late ministry at Melbourne. It might have been well deemed that he had transplanted his whole self, his hopes, aspirations, and affections to that new world. But no; all this career of honour and success seems but a pallid phantom in comparison with the memory of the days in which to him and his fellows the day-dawn of a liberated Ireland seemed near its breaking."

From THE DUBLIN EVENING MAIL.

Duffy, Davis, and Dillon, whatever opinions we may be inclined to take as to the precise benefit which each or any of them conferred upon his country, will long be remembered in Ireland, as sincere, high-minded, and lofty-spirited gentlemen. . . . We are unable now, as Sir Gavan Duffy shows the MAIL was unable forty years ago, to express our approval of the schemes put forward by the Young Ireland party; but on that account we cannot deny to the 'dauntless three' who broached that movement their legitimate place in the history of the men who, for one cause or another, Ireland has a right to be proud of."

From THE IRISHMAN.

"The utility of such a work is not measured by a

S

day or period; it will remain as a sort of political evangel for the guidance of generations, raising up the hearts and standards of the people, chastening the aspirations of a race, and transforming them into the noble instincts of a nation. It is a large and liberal donation to the country—this volume in which the mind is directed, by no swerving hand, along the high paths of patriotism, and enriched by the rare experience of honourable and successful statesmanship. . . . Each of them has, it is true, received his meed of appreciative praise, in Duffy's historical volumes—good measure, well pressed, and brimming over, with the one exception of the author himself. This should be remembered to him whose brain originated an Irish literature, whose reputation has been appreciated by men of honour who have suffered, like John O'Leary, and whose life history was summed up in the words of Charles Kickham: 'Duffy is the father of us all.'"

From THE BELFAST NORTHERN WHIG.

"There is no class of Irishmen who will not find much to interest them in the fascinating description and judicious criticisms of this book. The editor is dealing with the dead, and deals tenderly with their memory. . . . A marvellously interesting, and almost sensational story. It must be conceded that he has been remarkably fair and temperate in his criticism of men and events."

From THE CORK EXAMINER.

" This is by far the most valuable contribution to Irish history that we have had for a generation. It tells the story of a memorable epoch with a thorough knowledge of a man who bore in that epoch a great part, with the fairness of a generous nature dealing with friends and foes whose bones are dust, and with the grace, the brilliancy, and the lucid order of a master of literary style. . . . The writer's portraitures of two of the three greatest of the 'dramatis personæ'—O'Connell and Davis—are of high historical value. Of the third scarcely anything is said; and yet, of 'Young Ireland' he was the founder, the sagacious organiser, the brilliant chief—Charles Gavan Duffy himself. We cannot remember any narration of a series of events in which the narrator was also a chief actor so free of egotism as this. But of the other notabilities of the movement the book is rich with graphic traits."

From The Cork Herald.

"It has been said that men of genius never grow old, and the latest work of Sir C. Duffy is worthy of his prime—full, clear, and resonant with the unmistakable 'note of genius.' . . . The men themselves formed a rare combination. Davis, a Protestant of the South, the son of an officer of Artillery, was brought up amongst a family allied with the Established Church, and of strictly Conservative principles. Duffy was a Catholic from the North, and Dillon a Catholic from the West, who had pursued for some time ecclesiastical studies at Maynooth, and always retained the deep convictions, the seriousness of thought, and that charity of feeling and of manner, that would have made him an ornament to any priesthood. Here were elements combined that never before worked together for Ireland, and it was with this triad of intellects that Young Ireland arose, as the old Christianity of Ireland began with the three-fold leaf that has become our national emblem. . . . Wherever the Irish race has gone and its seed has been scattered broadcast over the earth, there, too, have Irish traditions gone, that were garnered by the NATION; there, too, the air vibrates with poetry that first crystallized into song in the pages of a journal that made a great reputation almost in a day, and worthily held it as long as it was worth the holding."

From THE MAIL, Sydney, New South Wales.

"The political work done was great, but the literary was even greater. The idea of this part of these young giants' labours was the creation of a great national literature, the revival of the lost glories, literary, religious, and historical, of old Ireland, and generally, in the language of their chief, 'the education of a people long depressed by poverty, or injustice, in fair play, public spirit and manliness.' It was a noble idea as nobly attempted; and as the leader, almost creator, of these splendid young spirits now sadly admits, far their wisest work and their best."

From THE NEWCASTLE DAILY CHRONICLE.

"He appropriately closes with the death of Davis. There are few things in the English language more delicately discriminative or more replete with tenderness than this prose elegy, which recalls all the freshness and power of Carlyle's tribute to Edward Irving. Time, which changes so much, has left Sir Charles Gavan Duffy's literary power untouched. Neither hand nor brain has forgot its cunning."